Sons of Lyra

Felicity Heaton

First printed March 2011

First Edition

Layout and design by Felicity Heaton

CONTENTS

SLAVE PRINCESS

Captain Lyra II, known as Balt to his family, is one of the famed sons of Lyra, the handsome princes with passionate hearts that every girl in the galaxy wants to catch. The second eldest son, he's content with the freedom and adventure that life in deep space and the Lyran Imperial Army offers him. What he isn't content with is the current situation he's found himself in. Not only has he been forced to stop at a backwater port for supplies, but he's leaving with more than he expected!

Kayla is a slave but can still vaguely recall what it had been like to be free. It's something she believes that she'll never taste again, and when she finds herself handed over like the piece of property she is to a complete stranger, a Lyran prince no less, she's convinced her life is about to get a lot worse. Taken onboard his ship, she quickly finds herself torn between fulfilling a promise she made to her friends when she was young, and falling for his chivalry and good looks.

Balt, not wanting a woman as his slave and not wanting to become the laughing stock of the admirals, intends to dump Kayla at the first decent planet he comes across, but as he starts to learn more about her, he finds it harder to fight his growing attraction to her. A passionate kiss from her only makes things worse. When Minervan mercenaries demand he hand her over, he discovers her true heritage and realises that things are more complicated than he'd believed.

Will Balt let her go, sending her into a life as a pleasure whore for the highest bidder, or will he fight to protect her? Will Kayla take revenge for her people, the Terrans, who were almost exterminated when Lyra destroyed the Earth system? Can love between a prince and an enslaved princess ever have a fairytale ending?

SLAVE PRINCESS

Two fingers rested on the muzzle of his laser pistol. His other hand held the inventory pad, thumb cycling through the screen of items they needed while the Sekarian trader who owned the store did his best attempt at flattery. Balt didn't listen to anything he had to say. All he wanted to do was get what they needed and get out.

He hated these backwater space ports but his ship, the Namrus-Lyra, needed supplies and it was too far to an imperial planet. His fingers tensed against the gun when something clattered to the dirty dark floor nearby and he shot around to see what had happened. A young woman went to pick up the items she'd dropped and then curled up into a tight ball with her hands over her head. His eyes widened when he realised that the man had left him and was heading over to her. His fingers locked around his pistol. Before the man had a chance to use the shock-stick on the woman, he'd pressed the muzzle of the pistol against the side of his ugly blue head.

"Leave her be or we're through doing business," he whispered, deadly and serious. He wasn't about to stand by and let a man beat a defenceless woman because she'd dropped something.

He really hated these backwater ports. They had no manners or breeding.

The man smiled and slipped the stick back into its holster. He babbled on about the lack of good hands in the port and other things that he didn't bother listening to. His concern was wholly with the woman. Bending over, he caught her around the upper arm and hauled her to her feet.

She immediately turned her face away from him, gathered the things she'd dropped, and hurried off.

Not exactly the appreciative response he'd expected. He'd saved her from a beating after all. She could have at least shown a little thanks. A smile would have done.

He finished checking off the inventory while the man continued to talk about supplies. A high pitched whine in his ear and a fizzing noise made him flinch. He tugged the translator out and glared at it. A thin column of smoke was coming out of the small sky blue device. He removed the secondary device from his throat. Without the translator working to detect the language being spoken to him, the voice alteration system wouldn't work—it wouldn't be able to change what he was saying into the appropriate language.

The man continued to talk. He could only pick up the occasional word. A cursory glance around him revealed that none of his crewmen had their translators on them and he knew none of them could speak Sekarian. He frowned as he listened hard, trying to catch the few words he'd learned during his tutelage on Lyra Prime. He wished his parents had let him have the memory injection he'd wanted for his twenty-first birthday. The knowledge of all those languages would have made his life a lot easier.

He tossed the broken translator and voice alteration device over his shoulder. There was a scuffle but he didn't look around. Lyran technology even in its broken state was worth a lot to the people who lived in places like this.

The man grinned at him, revealing a double set of broken and black teeth. Sekarian males really were a vulgar species—thin blue skin, rolls of fat, matted black hair and the worst hygiene he'd ever come across. He'd hate to see their women. He swallowed and smiled, taking the inventory pad back but never taking his hand off his pistol. The man gestured towards something and he looked across the cluttered low-lit room full of ship parts to see the woman he'd helped stand. The man said something with an ever-widening smile. He didn't understand a word of it. He smiled and nodded, wanting to get away and presuming the man was saying something about the fact he'd been kind enough to spare her a beating.

He handed the man two gold Lynans and then walked away, signalling for his men to join him. The man grabbed his arm. He turned on the spot with his pistol raised, a frown marrying his dark eyebrows. The man shook his head and said something. He cursed the broken translator. Did he want more money? He went to put his hand into the pouch at his waist to get more but then stopped when the man left him. He holstered his pistol and watched in fascination as the Sekarian grabbed the woman's arm and dragged her over. She struggled, whimpering and trying to prise the man's fingers off her.

When the man stopped in front of him with the woman, he didn't know what to do or say. It definitely wasn't more money he wanted. He looked around him again, desperate to find one of his crew that could understand what was happening and wanting nothing more than to get back on the ship as quickly as possible. All of his crew had gone off with the supplies, leaving him alone to deal with the shop owner.

"I don't understand."

The man grinned and lifted the woman's arms, prodding her curved sides and toned stomach. He frowned when the man squeezed the woman's breasts and the woman hung her head forward and tried to turn away, as though ashamed. The man muttered something and grabbed her jaw, forcing her head up. She looked at him with emerald eyes rimmed with long dark lashes. They would have been beautiful had there not been so much fear and disgust in them. The man squeezed his fingers into her cheeks, making her open her mouth. He gestured lewdly towards his crotch and the woman snapped out of his grip. The man grabbed her by her hair and dragged her back to him.

He'd had about enough of this. It was sickening to see this man parading the woman as though she was nothing but flesh for pleasure or profit. His hand went to his pistol.

"I wouldn't do that if I were you, Captain Lyra II."

He turned sharply to face the newcomer. A Minervan mercenary. It was easy to recognise one. The black and silver flight suit and malicious glint in the man's all-black eyes gave him away. His hand locked tight around his pistol but he didn't draw it. The Minervan man grinned at him, exposing the sharpened points of his glistening white teeth. If it weren't for such a disgusting habit as that, the Minervans would have been comparable to Lyrans in their beauty.

He'd hoped that no one would know him here. His heart thumped hard against his chest while he waited to see what would happen. The Minervan mercenaries loved nothing more than trying to kidnap him or his brothers. The ransom his parents, the king and queen of Lyra, would pay for their safe return would set them up as one of the foremost powers in the galaxy. They knew this and they were intent on getting their hands on the money one way or another. Not even the Minervan military were above attempting to kidnap them at times.

A few of his crew members returned, their guns instantly locked on the Minervan.

The Minervan smiled. "I'm not here to fight. I am here to amuse myself. My ship is in no state to battle yours."

"Amuse yourself how?"

"With your ignorance."

The Sekarian trader babbled something and his attention was back with him. The trader cupped the woman's crotch and she whimpered and tried to escape him. He turned his gun on the trader, torn between protecting himself and protecting her.

"I said I wouldn't do that... all that education must have gone to waste on you." There was a laugh in the Minervan's tone.

He'd learnt enough about the universe on Lyra Prime to spend years practicing the Minervan language so he'd never be in a situation with one where he didn't know what was going on.

"Why not?" he said.

The Minervan laughed and turned away. "Because you own her. The little whore is yours now. Another time, Captain Lyra II."

Balt stared at the woman. He owned her? When he got back to the ship, he was going to write an angry letter to the scientific institute on Lyra Prime. It was time they made him a translator that didn't break after barely a week's use.

"Captain, we must leave." The crewman nearest him gestured in the direction of the ship.

He continued to stare at the girl. The Sekarian grabbed the chain attached to the collar around her throat and held it around to him. He owned her? Had the man offered her along with the supplies? Did he think he wanted a pleasure slave?

He didn't.

The woman lowered her head so her matted long jet black hair covered her face. Her arms wrapped around herself. She looked so incredibly small and hurt. His eyes traced the numerous pale scars on her dirty flesh. He couldn't leave her here. The Sekarian would probably kill her if he did.

He took the chain, bowed stiffly to the man, and then turned towards the docks. He kept the chain tight at first, dragging her along with him at a swift pace, and then slowed once he was out of sight of the Sekarian. The chain slackened and he looked back at the woman. She was walking behind him, her head bowed and air subservient. He hadn't realised just how little clothing she was wearing. Nothing more than thin scraps of material covered her crotch and breasts. He wasn't going to enjoy walking onboard his ship with her. The scientific institute were going to get a very angry letter.

He ignored the jeers and wolf whistles of his crew as he walked up the ramp of his ship and through the corridors. A tinny echo followed him as he stormed towards the rear of the ship, his boots heavy on the black metal walkway. He opened a door at the end and went to enter.

The chain tightened and he turned to see the woman had braced her bare feet and hands against the doorway. He walked back to her. She gave him a fearful look and then her eyes flickered to the room. He looked at it, at the point where her eyes had darted to. The bed. When he looked back at her, she was shaking her head, spilling tears onto her cheeks.

"No... no... that's not why I brought you here," he said but she continued to shake her head.

Clearly she didn't understand. He growled in frustration and she flinched, curling up into a ball. He didn't have time for this. He wanted to be out of this system as soon as possible. There was no time for fooling around with translators and women.

Balt grabbed her, restrained her arms, and carried her through the room and into the bathroom. He dumped her down under the shower and turned it on, keeping hold of the chain that connected to the collar around her neck.

She hunched up, the warm water bouncing off her and plastering her hair against her face.

"Wash," he said and she gave him a confused look. He ran his fingers through his hair, cursed under his breath, and then leaned towards her. "Wash!"

He grabbed the soap dust and shoved it into her hand.

She still looked confused.

Hadn't she ever showered before? The amount of dirt on her said she probably hadn't. He wondered what she looked like underneath all that filth. Taking some of the dust, he ran it under the water a moment, until it became a gel and swelled up. He took a deep breath and then applied it to her shoulder. She tried to get away from him, dragging him into the shower and dousing him. He growled and tugged on the chain, wrapping it around his hand until she was forced to remain near him.

He rubbed a patch of her shoulder with the gel and was surprised when pale skin was revealed.

"Wash." He glanced into her eyes to make sure she understood now, took her hand and poured some of the dust onto it. It swelled up. She stared at it and then her gaze followed his hand and hers as he made her wash herself. "Wash."

She swallowed and nodded.

He was getting somewhere at least. He released his tight grip on her chain, letting it go slack.

His eyes widened when she stripped off her little tan coloured top and he turned his back on her. He stared at the far wall, trying to erase the sight of her round breasts from his mind. His cock twitched and his eyes slid to the mirror on the wall. She'd turned her back too. He struggled to keep his breathing level while he watched her washing, the soap suds skimming down the luscious curve of her bare back.

Dropping the chain, he left the bathroom and went straight to the door. He needed to get out of this system. He hated these backwater ports.

Balt closed the door to her room and locked it from the outside so she couldn't escape. He'd get one of the female officers to tend to her and bring her food and clothes. The less he had to do with her the better. At the first available and half-decent planet, he'd drop her off with a few gold Lynans and she'd be out of his life.

He walked up to the bridge and issued the order to leave as soon as they had everything onboard.

Before a handful of minutes had passed, they had blasted out of the atmosphere and were heading into deep space. It was several days journey to the nearest imperial army space station. Hopefully they could find somewhere to set the girl down en route. He didn't want to have to explain about her to the admirals at the space station. He'd be the laughing stock of the fleet. His brothers would never let it go.

He handed out orders to the crew on the bridge and then walked down the corridor towards the mess hall. The moment he entered, he looked around for a female crew member. There was only one. He recognised her as one of the co-pilots.

"You." He stormed towards her. "I presume word has spread quickly and you're aware that we picked up more than spare parts at that port?"

She nodded, her eyes showing her smile even when her lips weren't. He was already the laughing stock of his crew. Great. By Iskara's wings, the scientific institute were in for a beating.

"She's in the room by cargo bay three. Take some water to her, get her some clothes, do whatever needs to be done. Lock the door on your way out." He turned away before the woman had a chance to protest and went to his quarters.

The door slid shut behind him with a sigh and Balt walked across the room to his desk. He slumped into his chair, wiped his hands over his face as though that action alone could erase all his stress, and then pressed the button to open the shutters across the window. The black of deep space greeted him, comforting and reassuring as always. It was just a few days, possibly even less.

He poured himself a glass of sapphire blue Lyran Aquan, the strongest liqueur in the Lyra system, and leaned back into his seat.

His thoughts drifted to the woman.

Would she understand when he dumped her on some planet where she didn't know anyone?

Perhaps he should talk to her. She didn't look Sekarian or Minervan, and she didn't appear to be a Lyran. She hadn't spoken a word to him so it was hard to tell where in the universe she came from. She could be from any one of the humanoid species. He wondered if she'd talk to him even if he tried to talk to her. Could she talk?

In Iskara's name, how had she got herself stuck in that port as a slave anyway?

He remembered the Minervan and hoped that he wasn't going to be trouble. Even with running repairs to the ship, it was in no state for a battle. All he wanted was a quiet trip back to the nearest space station for maintenance and a break. It had been three months since they'd left Lyra Seven, the outermost planet in the system, and they'd faced nothing but battle after battle. He was weary of them now, and longing for the stretching blue skies and warm volcanic baths of his home world.

A little pampering wouldn't go amiss either.

Sometimes he thought his eldest brother, Sebastian, had things right. Stay at home on Lyra Prime and live a life of luxury and safety.

Other times, Balt wanted nothing more than to embrace the adventure and excitement that being a captain in the Lyran Imperial Army offered him.

Today, he just wanted to shut himself away until everything blew over, everything including the woman.

The door intercom buzzed.

"What is it?" he hollered.

"Sir," a female voice came through the speaker and he realised it was the woman he'd sent to check on their new guest. "I think you should come and see this."

He frowned, downed his drink, and was on his feet before she'd even finished her sentence. He opened the door and stared hard at her. He just wanted a quiet life.

"See what?" he said and then realised that the woman was holding her arm. There was a gash in the sleeve of her tight blue flight suit and he could see blood. "What happened?"

The woman looked at her arm and then back at him. "It seems she doesn't like me, sir."

"What did you do?" He couldn't believe that such a slight girl could have inflicted so much damage without intense provocation.

"I offered her some clothes... that's all. She took the water I gave, but when I tried to get her to dress, she turned wild. I had to run out of the door... she..."

"Enough." He walked past her, striding down through the corridors towards the woman's room. He'd find out firsthand what the problem was. It was time he had a little talk with his slave girl. "Get me two translators, quickly."

The woman nodded and broke away from him.

He opened the door to the girl's room and entered cautiously, his hand resting over his pistol. He flicked the dial down so it would only stun her if he was forced to use it. He didn't want to. Judging by the scars on her body, she'd suffered enough for several lifetimes. There was no need for him to add to her trauma unless she became life threatening.

The door closed behind him.

He scanned the room. There was no sign of her. The place was a mess. The blue silk covers had been torn off the double bed, the pillows tossed across the room. One of them had been split open, spilling the fine Friskin feathers inside. He edged further into the room. The table and chairs were tipped over. The vase near the window had been smashed, littering blue glass across the pale grey floor. He leaned to the side and peered towards the bathroom. She had to be in there. There was nowhere else for her to hide.

His steps were slow and measured, his breathing level and steady as he approached the bathroom. He pressed his back into the wall that separated the room from the corridor outside and slid towards the bathroom door. It opened to reveal an even bigger mess than was in the main room. Everything was scattered across the white glass floor—towels, beauty products, even what little clothing she'd been wearing before. Shards of the mirror created a dangerous assault course. The soap dust container had been left in the wet of the shower and had turned into a gelatinous blob. There was blood on the floor. He presumed it belonged to the poor woman he'd sent in to tend to the girl. The broken mirror explained how she'd got the cut. The girl must have used it as a weapon.

He eased inside the small room and frowned when he saw her.

She was curled up in the corner holding her knees to her chest. The chain attached to her collar snaked across the floor towards him, the end near his foot.

"Are you alright?" he said and she tensed, pulling her knees tighter against her chest. She looked so incredibly tiny.

Her black hair hid her face. Her skin was milky now that she was clean, tainted only by pinkish scars that hadn't healed yet.

"Are you alright?" Balt tried again. She buried her face into her knees and turned away so her side was facing him.

She couldn't understand him. She probably thought he was coming back to do all the terrible things to her that the Sekarian had spoken of. He crouched down near the door, keeping his distance. He had to get her out of the bathroom and dressed. There was no way he could have a conversation with her until she was in a decent state of dress. He'd never be able to concentrate and he would definitely give her the wrong impression, especially if his body kept reacting as it was now. He stifled his urges and stood.

Moving across the room, the shattered mirror pieces splintered under his heavy boots, crunching against the glass floor tiles.

The second he went to touch her arm, she launched herself at him, scratching down his face and pushing him backwards into the shower area of the room. He slipped on the wet tiles and went crashing to the ground. She bolted.

He was on his feet before she could make it halfway across the main room and grabbed her around the waist, lifting her off the floor. Her legs flailed, catching him hard in the crotch and killing any urges he might have had. He gritted his teeth, swallowed hard and tightened his grip on her.

She elbowed him in the face.

He threw her onto the bed and grappled with her until he was sitting astride her hips with his hands pinning hers to the bed.

She breathed hard and screwed her face up as she struggled again, trying to break free.

His eyes raked over her against his will. Her breasts heaved as she breathed and he tried to look away from them but couldn't. They were so tempting—luscious mounds peaked with hard dusky nipples. The door opened.

He looked across the room to see his first lieutenant standing in the doorway with the female co-pilot he'd sent to get the translators.

"I thought there might be trouble," the woman said in a quiet voice, a stunned look on her face.

That stunned look was echoed on his first lieutenant's face.

Balt knew how bad it looked. He was kneeling astride a naked woman after all. How good could it look?

"Just hurry up with those," he said to his first lieutenant when he saw the man was holding the translators.

The man hurried over to him and put the small device into his ear for him, and then into the woman's.

"Now leave," he said and was thankful when they did.

The woman looked up at him with wide green eyes. They sparkled at him. Beautiful.

"If I let go, will you behave yourself?" He hoped the translator would pick up her language when she spoke.

"I can understand you." The disbelief in her voice matched her expression.

"The thing he put in your ear is a translator. If I let you go?"

"Yes," she whispered and he released her. He went to the clothes that lay on the floor and picked them up.

"Put these on." He tossed them across the room to her and kept his back turned.

He tapped his toe impatiently and stared at the dull grey wall while she dressed. She was taking a long time. He wondered if it had been a while since she'd worn clothes.

"Done," she said and he turned back around to look at her.

She was truly beautiful without all the filth. She was sitting on the end of the bed, the tight blue flight suit hugging her lithe figure and undone to halfway down her chest. The material squashed her breasts together and formed a modest cleavage. He swallowed at the memory of how good they'd looked when she'd been below him. It had been too long since he'd had a woman, and she was more beautiful than any he'd had.

"Why did you attack me?" he said.

"I thought..." There was fear in her eyes again.

"I wouldn't do that to a woman." Balt paced across the room to the windows. He opened the shutters and her attention was immediately with the dark space outside.

She moved to the window and pressed her hands against the glass. He'd never seen anyone look so fascinated before. When she looked at him, there was a smile in her eyes.

"It's been a long time since you left the port," he said and she nodded before looking back out of the window. "How long have you been working down there?"

"Working?" She snorted in contempt. "I'm a slave."

"Not anymore."

She scowled at him. "I still am a slave. He gave me to you because he thought you liked me... he thought you wanted me. Don't you want me?"

He frowned. His better sense said to deny her words, even though they were true. He did want her. Something drew him to her, lured him in until he could only think of her.

"How long have you been a slave?" He chose to ignore what she'd said.

"As long as I can remember really." She pulled the translator from her ear. "How does this work?"

"It's Lyran technology—" He cut himself off when she looked confused and sighed as he put the device back into her ear. "It's Lyran technology. It knows all languages of the universe and can automatically translate them."

Her brows rose. "Lyran. You're a Lyran... and you're speaking Lyran? And I can understand you because of this?"

He nodded.

"What language are you speaking?" Balt said, figuring it was a better way of asking her where she was from than asking outright.

"In the port, you couldn't understand him... but you understood the other man... you spoke a different language to him."

"Minervan. Pray to Iskara that that other man, as you put it, doesn't follow us. We're in no shape for another battle with him." He caught hold of her hand when she went to take the translator out of her ear again. She could look at it all she wanted later. Right now, she was going to answer his questions. "What language are you speaking? It's not Sekarian or Minervan, or anything that I recognise."

She flashed a smile and hopped onto the bed. He looked at her where she knelt on the pillows, staring out of the window. He was beginning to get the impression she didn't like answering questions.

"What planet did you call home?" he said, losing patience.

She looked at him with wide beautiful eyes. "I never had a planet to call home."

He frowned and walked over to her, sitting down beside her on the bed. His hand remained close to his pistol. She'd already cut him once because he'd tried to get too close. Just because she was speaking to him didn't mean he was about to let his guard down.

"No planet. Do you know what language you're speaking?" He held her gaze. A hint of sadness entered hers.

She was quiet for a moment as she turned away and stared off into the distant darkness.

"Terran," she whispered.

Terran? The Earth system. She was a Terran. He'd never met one before. Most never did. They had been scattered to the four winds when their system had been destroyed.

It had been destroyed by his great great grandfather.

"You knew I was Lyran." He watched her closely for any sign of a reaction to the name of the species that had killed so many of hers.

"I knew," she said with a small, joyless smile. "At least I suspected as much and then I heard the Minervan call you Captain Lyra II... which makes you royalty."

"And makes you more informed than I thought."

Kayla gave him a real smile this time. She'd figured he'd think her an ignorant and uneducated woman. Just because she'd been forced into slavery didn't mean she hadn't been raised well. She could remember her parents. She knew the story of how the Lyrans had destroyed her home world and that they could never return there. They were orphans of space like so many others whose systems had been caught up in wars. Earth hadn't been in direct conflict with either the Lyrans or the Vegans. It had merely been in the way of their fight.

She looked at him as he stared out of the window. Never in all her short years had she imagined that the one species she hated above all would be the one species to rescue her. Now she didn't know how to feel. He was royalty.

Her parents had told her of the current rulers and their children, the famed sons of Lyra, handsome from the day they were born. When she was younger, she'd made a pact with her friends Tyla and Serena. If they ever met a Lyran, they'd get revenge for their species.

Back then things had been simple.

Back then the Lyran in question hadn't been her rescuer.

And he hadn't been so gorgeous.

Now she didn't know how to feel.

He touched his cheek and the scratches she'd inflicted. A smile curved his beautiful bow lips. Amusement shone in his dark eyes but was quickly replaced by a serious look.

"Is this why you attacked me?"

"I was defending myself." She would have done a lot worse if she'd wanted to hurt him and get revenge. His pistol had been within easy reach. She could have taken it and killed him. Why hadn't she? She reasoned that it was because she was on a Lyran ship and had no chance of escaping it alive if she killed him.

The voice at the back of her head said that it was because he'd rescued her. She felt as though she was caught between a terrible reality and a beautiful fantasy. Why had he had to rescue her and why did he have to be a prince? Now she couldn't stop imagining he was a knight of old in shining armour.

Kayla looked him over. Not quite armour and she was sure that when her grandmother had whiled away the dark hours with her that the armour she'd spoken of wasn't quite as revealing as his flight suit.

"Are you going to keep me?" She was painfully aware that she was his property now. He could do whatever he wanted with her. Why wasn't he? She wasn't naive or blind. She'd seen the hunger in his eyes when he'd been on top of her.

He shook his head and she frowned when a strange feeling of disappointment swept through her.

"What will you do with me?" She turned to face him.

His eyes met hers again, sending a warm rush through her.

"I will set you down on a planet between here and the space station we're destined for."

There was no emotion in his voice or in his expression. He would set her down. Just like that. He didn't care what happened to her really. He was a typical Lyran after all.

"Fine." Kayla looked back out of the window. So what if he didn't want to keep her. She didn't want him to be her master anyway. She'd find a job on the planet he dumped her on, save enough to buy a rusty old space ship, track him down and fly it into his fancy fighter ship in the hopes of killing him. Her gaze flicked to his pistol. The pact she'd made was starting to sound possible after all. If only he'd take his hand away from his gun.

He stood and paced across the room.

Her gaze ran down his body and her thoughts betrayed her again. He really had looked after himself. The flight suit left nothing to the imagination. Every muscle was outlined for her pleasure. He turned back to face her, his hands clasped behind him. Her stomach warmed. Every muscle.

She raised her eyes to his face. She could see why half the galaxy spoke of the sons of Lyra as though they were gods. He was handsome, his dark hair and brows setting off the equal darkness of his eyes, and his straight nose and bowed lips making him appear as regal as she knew he was.

"It will probably be a day or so before we reach a suitable planet," he said and Kayla wished he hadn't spoken.

She'd been happily lost in a fantasy and he'd had to ruin it by reminding her that he intended to ditch her.

"You should have left me back there." She got to her feet, went to the row of windows and leaned against the grab rail that ran at waist height along them.

"He would have killed you."

"I know." She leaned forwards, folding her arms and resting her chin on them.

"You'd rather die than be free?" He stood beside her. She could feel his gaze boring into her face. She didn't look at him.

She didn't say a word.

There was nothing to say. The Sekarian probably would have killed her, but it sounded like a better fate than being dumped on some distant dreary planet. She gave it a week before she was someone else's slave or worse. This time she'd probably end up on one of the pleasure planets, doped up to her eyeballs and too out of it to fight the disgusting men pawing at her.

Taking the translator out of her ear, she straightened and looked at him. She took his hand, turned it palm up and placed the device into it.

She'd rather not understand a word he was saying when everything he said only hurt her.

Lying down on the bed, she rolled over so she was facing away from him and curled up holding her chain in her hands.

He said something that sounded a lot like curse words and then stormed out of the room. She heard the locks on the door slide into place. For someone who said she was free and didn't belong to anyone, he certainly wanted to keep her captive.

Closing her eyes, Kayla tried to remember her family and where she'd come from. She did this every time she finally had a chance to rest. It was important to remember her heritage. There were hardly any Terrans left now. Her friends had all been killed in a Vegan attack on the space station they'd lived on with her. She'd been taken into slavery with some others. She screwed her face up, not wanting to remember all the dark times she'd been through since then. She'd never thought she'd escape that last planet. Now she was on a Lyran ship heading away from it, but there was no comfort.

He was going to ditch her at the first opportunity.

A slave like her wasn't good enough for a prince like him.

He didn't even want to touch her.

Was she that repulsive to him?

It wasn't long before she'd drifted off to sleep. She only realised she had when she heard a noise and opened her eyes to see that the man had returned. She watched him right the table and chairs, and place a tray of food down on the round table. He held the translator device up and said something before setting it down beside the tray. Why did he care so much about her speaking to him? He was going to drop her off any time now. It made more sense for him to just keep her shut in the room and ignore her.

He sat down, an impatient look on his face as he stared at a computer pad similar to the one he'd had at the port. He frowned and muttered something. She cursed him for making her want to put the translator back in so she could understand him. Her stomach growled when she looked at the food.

She'd not seen fresh food in years.

Slipping off the bed, she padded quietly across the room and stared at the food. There was fruit. Where had he got fruit? Did all the crew on his ship get such luxurious food, or was it his personal supply he was offering to her?

She sat down, her eyes still fixed on the fruit and her mouth watering as she remembered how delicious the only fruit she'd ever tasted had been. It had been a bruised apple core that she'd found discarded on a space port floor when her family had been travelling to their second home—the last home she'd had.

This fruit wasn't bruised. It was perfect and shiny. There were beautiful red quarib berries and rich green polans apples. It was fruit she'd stared at so many times in the shop windows of the ports she'd passed through or been a slave at. She'd never thought she'd get to eat something so luxurious.

She looked at the man. He paused at his work and gestured for her to eat. She flexed her fingers, grabbed everything she could, and ran across the room to the bed. Curling up in the corner of it furthest from him, she could feel the man's eyes on her. She brushed the chain dangling from her neck away and clutched the fruit to her chest when he walked over, unwilling to share it now that she had it. She could live for weeks on this much food.

"Mo kullinso terra yoi erasu." He smiled at her and held his hand out.

She looked at the device sitting on the middle of his palm. She thought about swatting it away and then sighed. Taking the device, she pushed it back into her ear.

"That's better," he said with a wider smile. "Isn't it better when you can understand me?"

"I'll never understand you," she muttered into her food and then bit into one of the apples. It was juicy and sweet. She moaned and bit into it again and again, until her mouth was so full she couldn't chew.

He laughed and she scowled at him, making him stop.

"I'm sorry... I've never seen someone eat fruit with such... such... hunger." His expression changed as he said that last word, concern surfacing in his eyes with a trace of fear. Was he worried that he'd said something wrong?

He looked her over.

"I haven't eaten in almost two weeks, if that's what you're trying to figure out." She ate the remains of the apple and swallowed it down. "You'd eat like this too if you knew what it was like to be hungry. I bet you've never been hungry in your life."

He frowned at her, a dark look entering his eyes. She knew she was pushing him. He deserved to be pushed. He'd probably lived the pampered life of luxury. He probably didn't have a clue about the terrible kinds of things she'd been put through. He shifted on the bed and her gaze lowered to his neck. There were several scars streaking down it, from the corner of his jaw to around the back of his neck. The more she looked at him, the more scars became evident. There was one to the side of his right eye, a dark one that said it had been a bad wound when it had happened. Maybe he did know of pain, but no amount of pain could be comparable to the things she'd experienced.

Kayla scoffed some of the berries to distract herself from her dark thoughts. One of them fell down her top. She dipped her fingers in and went to pull it out, but stopped when she realised that he was watching her. A furtive glance revealed his eyes were fixed on her hand where it was down her flight suit. She drew the berry up slowly, tracing her skin with it and teasing the curve of her left breast. His lips parted.

Perhaps he did want her. His eyes had said as much when he'd been on top of her and when he'd watched her in the shower.

"I can fulfil that desire," she said and his eyes shot up to meet hers.

"What desire?" he snapped with venom in his voice. She'd flustered him now.

She smiled and ran the berry a little higher towards her neck before tracing it along her lower lip and then sucking it into her mouth along with her fingers. She sucked them a moment, her eyes never leaving his. His narrowed and darkened again, but this time it was hunger in them, not anger.

She pulled her fingers free of her mouth with a pop. "That desire."

He glared at her and then stared out of the window.

She leaned back on the bed, intent on getting him to admit that he did want her.

"Come, Captain," she whispered with a smile. "You own me after all... you don't want to inspect the goods? You don't want one little taste before you drop me off? Your family would never know you'd been with a Terran... I'm clean."

His gaze shot to meet hers again. She couldn't read it now. There were too many conflicting feelings in it. She'd always been good at reading people, she had to be to avoid getting hurt worse than she had been, but he was beyond her capabilities. She'd never met a Lyran before. Perhaps it was his species and not just him.

She picked up another berry and caressed her breasts with it. "You don't want a taste?"

He frowned at her and took a deep breath. She'd never seen someone look so offended before.

"I have to do your bidding... I'm yours... you own me."

He stood sharply, his frown intensifying. "Stop saying that!"

Kayla was taken aback by the force of his words. Earlier he'd said that she wasn't his, that she wasn't a slave anymore.

"Does it offend you that you own me... that you can do anything with me that pleases you? I'm yours to command, Captain Lyra II. You won't touch me but I'm not stupid... I know you want to... so why don't you?"

He paced across the room, keeping his back to her. "You are not my property. You belong to no one but yourself. You are free."

"You didn't answer my questions." She stood and followed him across the room.

"I... it does offend me that someone thought to make you a slave and you believe you are one still."

She moved around him until he was facing her. He looked at her, right into her eyes. There was so much passion in them.

"And my other question?" She cocked her head to one side.

He paused, drew a deep breath, and then whispered, "Because it is wrong."

She would've laughed at that but he was so serious and solemn. She looked at him a moment, studying his expression and his eyes. He really did believe that it was wrong of him to want her.

"Because I'm a slave, or because I'm a Terran?" Kayla moved closer to him. She wanted to know which it was. Something was holding him back and she was determined to find out what it was. Disgust? Fear? Loathing? It had to be something other than self-control.

"You're not a slave," he said. "You're free."

She grabbed the chain attached to her collar, raised it up so he noticed it and then gave it a sharp tug. "I'm not free!"

"Why haven't you taken that off?" he said with a concerned frown.

She laughed now. "I can't. When the Sekarian handed you the chain, the collar took your DNA imprint. Only you can remove it because you own me."

The muscles in his jaw tensed at those last three words. He really was repulsed by the idea that he owned her. Most men in the universe would have been pleased. They would have been abusing her by now. Not this man though. All he wanted to do was free her. He thought he was doing that by setting her down on some random planet. He really was ignorant to the way the universe worked. From the moment he ditched her, it would be just a matter of time before someone else caught her and put her back into slavery. She was valuable. He didn't realise that.

His fingers brushed hers as he took the chain from her and she stood mute as he slid his other hand around the side of the collar and flicked the latches. A tremendous sensation of freedom and happiness filled her when the weight of the thick leather and steel collar disappeared from around her neck. She looked up into his eyes as he moved closer and the feelings inside her altered when he stroked her neck and the scars she knew were there.

He was so close.

Her eyes fell to his mouth and her lips parted.

She wanted to kiss him.

Just a brief kiss of thanks for setting her free.

That's all it was.

Her eyes met his again.

She pressed her hands into his chest to steady herself, tiptoed, and closed her eyes as her lips touched his. It was as brief as she intended, nothing more than a brushing of lips. She set back on her heels and took her hands away. He was staring at her now with fire in his dark eyes. His breathing was as heavy as her own.

"Will you kiss me now I'm not a slave," she whispered, holding his gaze and trying to read him. "Or is it because I'm a Terran?"

Her eyes widened when he grabbed her waist and dragged her up against his hard body. His lips crushed hers in a passionate kiss that made her heart skip a beat. She closed her eyes and leaned into it, wanting to feel his strength and his heat. Before, she'd wanted him to kiss her so she could prove to him that he wanted her. Now, she just wanted him to kiss her.

His tongue brushed hers as she licked his lips and she held back a moan when his hands, rough and strong, coursed up her back and pulled her harder against him. She was out of her mind. He kissed across her jaw, his breath hot and heavy in her ear. She decided that she didn't care. So what if she was giving him the impression that he could have her if he wanted her.

He could.

Something about him made it impossible for her to deny him. She wanted him. She'd wanted him from the second he'd touched her in that dirty port town.

Something buzzed.

Balt rolled his eyes and released the woman. In Iskara's name, what was he thinking? She wasn't his slave or his whore, but he was treating her as though she was. He stepped away from her and ran a hand over his hair.

"What is it?" he said to the quiet room filled only with their dual panting.

Damn he wanted to kiss her again. He'd never tasted anything as sweet and tempting.

She looked confused.

"Bridge to Captain Lyra II, we have company." The voice crackled over the intercom panel beside the door. The woman looked less confused.

"Company?" He turned towards the door. His heart jumped into his throat. They couldn't have caught up with them so quickly.

"The Minervans want the woman."

Balt frowned over his shoulder at her. She looked frightened now. They wanted her? Why?

He grabbed her arm and dragged her along behind him as he walked to the bridge. The Minervans usually fired first and asked questions later. Why was today so different? What did they want with the woman? Was she so important that they wouldn't risk firing upon them? They attacked his ship regardless of himself being onboard. Did they value her more than him?

The door to the bridge slid open with a swish and then closed behind them.

"On screen," he said to the communications officer.

The middle glass window of the bridge darkened and then the Minervan appeared on it.

"Captain Lyra II." The Minervan smiled winsomely. It was the man from the port. "Give me the girl and your ship won't be harmed."

Balt glared at him and walked forward with the woman. His hand tightened around her wrist when she tried to get away.

"What do you want with her?" he said.

The Minervan laughed, revealing his sharpened teeth. The woman tensed.

"You're so ignorant, Lyran. You don't know what you have." The Minervan's attention drifted to the woman.

Balt looked at her. There was so much fear in her eyes, more than he'd ever seen.

"I would've thought your filthy Lyran hands would've been all over her by now... but you must be a fool as well as ignorant... to waste such goods," the Minervan said with a lewd look at the woman. "Check the back of her neck and tell me what you see."

Balt pulled the woman towards him and turned her around. He brushed her hair over her shoulder and frowned when he saw the black intricate mark on the back of her neck. He knew that mark. The woman stepped away and looked over her shoulder at him, a pleading expression on her face.

"So you see, dear Captain... we want her... hand her over and we'll leave quietly."

He stared into the woman's emerald eyes. He couldn't do that to her.

"No deal. I own her. She's my property now." Balt slammed his fist down on the communications panel. The screen went dark and then cleared to reveal nothing but space. He turned to his crew, never relinquishing his grip on the woman's arm. "Change course. Set coordinates for Lyra Prime."

He dragged the woman with him as he headed back to her room. She had some questions to answer. His blood boiled when he thought about how close he'd been to falling for her trick. How dare she use her beauty against him? How dare she make him feel as though she really wanted him?

The door to her room slid open and he threw her inside. She hit the table and landed on her backside on the floor. She sat there, looking up at him with disbelief in her eyes.

He sneered at her.

"Did you intend to kill me?" he shouted at her. She flinched away and shook her head. "I don't believe you. You would've killed me!"

He grabbed her upper arm and roughly hauled her onto her feet. She lowered her head away from him and then slowly looked up at him.

"I wouldn't have," she whispered, her voice shaking with fear. "I should to avenge my people, but I didn't intend to."

He didn't know whether to believe her. If she was lying, she was incredibly good at it. From where he was standing, she looked sincere.

"Tell me." His grip on her arm increased. She cringed and whimpered. "How does Terran royalty become a slave?"

She hit him hard in the chest and broke free of his grasp. She backed away, rubbing her arm. Tears filled her eyes and he regretted his actions. She didn't deserve his anger. His heart said she hadn't been out to kill him. She'd wanted that kiss as much as he had.

"Only the mark saved me from death and made me valuable. The Vegans killed all my friends and killed my family before they realised who they were. Only I was left." She backed up against the wall and slid down it, curling up and holding her knees to her chest as she sobbed.

He walked over to her and crouched down.

"What does the Minervan want with you?"

She laughed. "You really are ignorant just as he said. I'd be worth a lot on the pleasure market... the last surviving member of Terran royalty... he'd sell me to the highest bidder as a whore."

He braced himself when the ship rocked. The Minervans weren't going to give up easily now that they knew he had her onboard. They wanted their prize as usual, but for once it wasn't him.

He looked at her, his chest aching to see the tears streaking her face.

"What are you going to do?" she whispered.

Another blast shook the ship.

She reached out and touched his arm. "If you hand me over, the Minervan will leave you alone."

He couldn't believe she'd just said that. She was willing to sacrifice herself in order to save his ship. He shook his head.

"I won't do that. A few more minutes and the coordinates will be set and we'll be able to lose them when we go into sub-space." He placed his hand over hers.

She looked down at it, her expression blank, and then looked back into his eyes.

"My family destroyed your world," he said. "I have to repay that debt and protect you."

Her eyes widened into a stunned look. "You're not going to ditch me?"

"No." He shook his head again. The plan to ditch her had been ridiculous even before the Minervan had shown up, a ploy to get her out of his sight and his thoughts. Now it was insane. He couldn't set her down anywhere. He had to protect her. "I will take you to Lyra Prime and my parents... and I will speak to them."

Her eyes widened further when another blast rocked the ship. There was genuine fear in their green depths. He curled his fingers around hers and held her hand. With his other hand, he pressed the button on the wristband he wore.

"Captain to the bridge. How are we doing with those coordinates? It's getting bumpy back here." His eyes never left hers. He squeezed her hand, hoping to reassure her that everything was going to be alright.

She swallowed and screwed her eyes shut when the ship shook. There was a high whine and the front cannons fired. At least his crew had found the good sense to retaliate while they waited. He was going to have to have words when all this was over.

Another blast hit the ship and the woman was in his arms, curled up with her head against his chest. He'd never met a woman so changeable in all his life. He released her hand and wrapped his arm around her, unable to resist this chance to touch her again.

"Ready now." Came the reply from the bridge.

Balt closed his eyes, rested his chin on top of her head, and held onto her tightly as the ship jerked and the sub-space engines kicked in. His head spun and his stomach turned. It was never pleasant making the transition between space and sub-space.

"What was that?" she said, still buried in his arms.

He knelt beside her and peeled her off him. Dipping his head, he looked up into her eyes. They searched his, pleading him to reassure her. He smiled and brushed the hair from her face. She really was beautiful, and that kiss had been electric. It had made him realise just how much he wanted her.

"Just the engines making the switch. We'll be approaching the Lyra system before two days have passed."

She uncurled and looked around her. Her gaze settled on the windows. He looked there, at the lights streaming past in a constant blurred line. When he went to look back at her, she was on her feet and moving past him. His eyes followed her as she walked towards the windows. He wondered if she'd ever travelled through sub-space. Not many ships had technology capable of it.

"What's your name?" She looked over her shoulder at him. A smile graced her lips and her cheeks coloured. Was she embarrassed to ask? She hadn't blushed when she'd kissed him.

"Captain Lyra II." He couldn't help teasing her, knowing that she already knew his title. He smiled too. "Balt."

"Balt?" she said and he nodded. "I'm Kayla."

Kayla. A beautiful name for a beautiful woman. He remained kneeling on the floor, staring up at her, not afraid of the comfortable silence between them. Looking at her now, he couldn't believe that he'd thought she'd been out to kill him. There was so much desire in her eyes, so much honesty in them too.

She walked slowly back towards him and sat on the end of the bed near him. He turned so he was facing her but remained on the floor at her feet.

The last of Terran royalty.

She was beautiful enough to be a princess. She was more beautiful than any princess he'd met.

"Balt?" Kayla said, slightly unnerved by his staring at her with such fire in his eyes. What was he thinking in there? She wanted to ask him but was too afraid of what the answer might be. "What will you do with me now?"

"Nothing. You're free... you don't belong to me. All that back on the bridge was just to throw the Minervan. You're not my property, Kayla. You belong to no one but yourself."

Her chest warmed at his words and the soft way he'd spoken her name. His expression was tender, eyes narrowed slightly on hers and his focus so intent that she felt as though she was the only other person in the universe with him.

"Doesn't your crew need you on the bridge?" she said, her nerves getting the better of her. She didn't want him to leave but she couldn't handle much more of this meaningful silence. It spoke words to her that made her feel strange. The longer he continued to be close to her like this, the more she began to realise just how attracted to him she was.

And just how attracted to her he was.

He shook his head. "They don't need me to fly the ship."

"You said it was two days to Lyra Prime... what do you intend to do in all that time?" She wished she hadn't said it when he rose on his knees and moved closer to her. His eyes narrowed on hers. She knew exactly how he intended to pass the time. She cursed the fact that she wasn't strong enough to stop him. Regardless of how attracted to him she was, he was still a Lyran, a son of Lyra no less. She shouldn't be having these feelings.

"Kayla," he whispered, voice low and husky, full of so much desire that she couldn't help looking at him. He nudged her knees apart and settled between them, his hands trailing fire as they brushed over them and came to rest on her thighs. "You asked me once if I wanted you."

She already knew the answer to that question but she got the impression that he needed to say it. He needed to admit that he wanted her—a Terran and a slave. She understood. She was having a hard time admitting that she wanted a Lyran and a prince.

He leaned forwards, spreading her legs further with his hips, and his hands reached her backside. It felt too good to have his hands on her, dangerously good.

His mouth neared hers and her eyes fell closed against her will. She struggled to maintain level breathing as anticipation coiled in her stomach.

Was he going to kiss her and put her out of her misery, or was he just going to torture her with the idea?

"I want you," he breathed against her lips. "Do you want me too?"

She couldn't find her voice. Of course she wanted him. She just couldn't bring herself to say it. She craved him more than food and water, more than the feel of the sun on her skin or the wind of freedom on her face. She needed him more than air itself.

Unable to speak, she swallowed and nodded.

His lips met hers, tender and soft, gentle enough to tell her that he'd witnessed her silent reply. She felt light inside, dizzy. She'd never been kissed with so much reverence and affection. Her only experience had been rough and brutal, and against her will. Did he know that? Was that why he was treating her so carefully?

She leaned forwards, wanting to deepen the kiss. Her tongue swept along his lips and he opened his mouth, his tongue coming to play with hers. It sent tingles sweeping down her spine and she sighed.

His hands moved to her waist, fingers pressing in slightly as she kissed him. She wanted to touch him too. She hesitated a moment and then placed her hands on his shoulders. He stopped kissing her and moved back. She met his gaze and then looked at her hands. Her heart hammered. Her mouth turned dry.

Her hands shook as she ran her fingers lightly down his arms, tracing the shape of his biceps. Her gaze slid across to the zipper on his flight suit. It was done up to his neck, the short stand up collar hiding part of it. She licked her lips and then moved her hand to it. One hand held the collar while her other slowly lowered the zip. She sighed quietly and her stomach heated through when the material parted to reveal his collarbones and then his chest. Her other hand left the collar, her fingers grazing his chest as she lowered them to follow the zipper.

He closed his eyes.

She'd never seen such quiet pleasure on a man's face before.

She lowered the zip to his navel and then coursed her hands back up, over the taut muscles of his abdomen to his chest. When she reached it, she slipped them underneath his flight suit and pushed it towards his shoulders. He helped her, peeling it off his arms and leaving it dangling at his waist. Her eyes drank their fill of his body. The sons of Lyra really were as perfect as she'd heard. At least Balt was.

Leaning forwards, she pressed light tentative kisses to his chest and neck, exploring his body—rock hard square pectorals, taut shoulders, and deliciously curved abdominals. He kept still, only his head moving slightly to the side when she kissed the spot below his square jaw line. Her whole body ached with desire and instinct drove her forwards, making her touch and kiss him to fulfil the need growing inside her. She wanted more.

Her gaze lowered to his navel and followed the line of dark hair downwards until it disappeared into the flight suit. She swallowed again as she wondered just how perfect a son of Lyra was. Something told her she'd find out if she found the courage to go through with what she wanted to do. He wouldn't stop her. She could already see the hardness of his cock against the tight material.

She looked at his face, checking his eyes were still closed. Her fingers skimmed his waist, ghosting lightly over the muscles there, and then dipped downwards. His lips parted and a small frown knit his brows.

Her fingers met at the point where she'd unzipped him to. She took a deep breath to calm her nerves and then carefully lowered the zipper to reveal dark snug trunks. She wanted to see more. He was going to have to stand.

She took hold of his hands and stood, forcing him to rise with her. He towered over her, his head bent towards her. She couldn't resist the opportunity to kiss him. Tiptoeing, she claimed his mouth as her own, plundering it passionately with her tongue. He moaned and a chill chased over her skin. When he did that, she wanted to do even more, she wanted to do whatever it took to make him moan again.

She pushed the flight suit down over his hips. He stepped backwards and removed his boots before stripping off the flight suit. Her gaze raked over him, absorbing the sight of his long powerful legs and the beauty of his body.

His hand reached out towards her. Her heart skipped a beat and she kept still as his fingers closed around the zipper on her flight suit. She bit her lip and watched him lower it, revealing her breasts and stomach, and then continuing downwards to her crotch. She didn't have the advantage that he did. She had no underwear on and he'd already seen her naked.

That fact didn't stop his eyes from filling with dark hunger as he peeled the suit off her body. She let him remove it for her, not wanting to interrupt the obvious pleasure he was getting from undressing her. He pushed the suit down her legs and came to kneel before her. She lifted each of her feet in turn so he could remove it completely. When he was done and she was naked, he looked up at her.

Her pussy throbbed, her nipples hardening at the dirty thoughts coursing through her mind.

He skimmed his hands back up her legs, tickling her and stirring intense need and desire inside her. She watched his hands and then his face, staring into his eyes. In them, she could see how much this meant to him, and it was far more than she'd expected. He really had wanted her. He did want her. She closed her eyes when he pressed a kiss to her thigh and then kissed across her stomach, his tongue laving her skin and making it tingle.

His hands cupped her backside.

Hers ran over his hair, holding him against her stomach. She'd never felt such pleasure before and it surprised her that it could come from something as innocent as a kiss.

"Kayla," he whispered up at her.

She looked down at him, realising for the first time that she had a man on his knees, subservient. No, not just a man. She had a prince of Lyra on his knees and he wore a look that said he would die if she welcomed him inside her. She ran her fingers around his earlobe and then under his jaw. Reaching his chin, she lifted her fingers and was amazed when he followed her silent command and stood.

Her tongue brushed his skin again, exploring his chest. He sighed and caught hold of her waist. She fell backwards onto the bed with him on top of her. His crotch pressed against hers, his lips coursing over her neck and downwards. She stretched her arms out above her head on the bed and closed her eyes, giving herself over to her desire and him.

His lips closed around her left nipple and he gave a gentle pull on it. She arched her back against him and moaned. Before she knew what she was doing, she had her legs wrapped around his waist and had bunched the bed sheets up into her fists.

"Balt," she breathed, his name unsteady on her lips. She wanted more, wanted him to touch her all over, taking her out of this universe and into one of their own making. She screwed her eyes shut when his tongue flicked and swirled around her nipple, torturing her. "Balt..."

He grabbed her hips and ground against her, powerful and rough. She moaned again and rubbed her pussy against his hard cock. The friction was exquisite. She wished she could feel his cock against her, its silken flesh sliding against her slick pussy. He thrust again, catching her clit and making it pulse with pleasure.

He kissed across to her other breast, laving and suckling the nipple until it was so taut that it hurt. She ran her hands down his back, pressing her fingers in hard in the hopes of driving him on. The tattered threads of her control began to slip through her grasp. She wanted to feel his cock against her. She needed it.

Tugging him upwards, she got him high enough that she could reach the dark trunks that formed the barrier between her and what she wanted. She pushed them down, her eyes immediately on his cock as it sprang free. He stood and removed his trunks for her. Her eyes widened at the length of his hard cock as he drew a hand down it to reveal the sensitive crown. She licked her lips.

Before she could move towards him to get a taste, he'd knelt before her at the end of the bed and had spread her thighs. She flung her head back and moaned loudly as his thumbs parted her pussy lips and brushed against her clit, quickly followed by his tongue. Her fingers closed around the sheets and her thighs tensed as he licked her, flicking the pert nub and sending her out of her mind. She bit her tongue to stop herself from moaning as loudly, fearing someone would hear. His tongue delved lower, probing her entrance and making hot shivers of need explode inside her. She grabbed his hair with one hand and arched her back. He placed her legs over his shoulders and drew her towards him until her backside was almost off the bed. She pressed her feet into his shoulders and spread her legs, encouraging him to continue. She needed more.

He slid a finger down her slick pussy and then eased it up into her. Her breath escaped her in a sigh as she felt the slightest sense of satisfaction and her hunger abated. He pumped her slowly with his finger as he licked her clit, sending tingles through her that built until she was riding his finger, unable to stop herself.

She came with a harsh moan, fireworks exploding behind her closed eyes and her pussy clenching his finger as he continued to thrust it inside her. She rode it still, not wanting to relinquish it or the delicious feeling of it being in her.

His movements slowed and his tongue caressed her clit, steadily teasing her and arousing her again. She kept her feet pressed against his shoulders but the hand that had been against his hand fell away to the bed. He looked up at her, his finger still inside, stroking her gently.

She stared into his hungry eyes for a moment and then down at his body. She couldn't see his cock but she knew it would be hard and ready. There was a look in his eyes that said when the time came, he wouldn't be gentle. There was too much passion and desire to control. She didn't mind. He'd been gentle enough. Now she wanted to feel his full strength.

He moved upwards and her feet slid down his back. He kept them hooked over him and she watched his cock come into view. He stroked a hand down it and her lips parted. She wanted it inside her. She pulled him towards her with her feet, encouraging him. He knelt closer to her and held himself poised at her entrance. She moaned when he ran the head of his cock over her pussy and then downwards. It nudged her slick opening, edging inside her and stretching her. She locked eyes with him as he eased in, deeper than she'd expected and filling her. Her legs stayed over his shoulders and she shifted forwards until he was as deep as he could go, his balls against her backside. His eyes closed for a brief moment and he took hold of her hips.

She groaned when he pulled out and then rammed back into her, sending fire into her veins. He stared at her, his eyes narrowed and intent as he thrust into her, hard and fast at first, frantic. His pace slowed but each plunge into her was deep and hard. His pelvis hit her clit, slamming into it and making her head spin. She moved her feet so her thighs were further apart and each brush of her clit was more intense. Her breasts wobbled as he pounded into her but she refused to close her eyes. She kept them fixed on his, staring into them, lost in their coupling and the feelings she could see surfacing inside him.

His breathing turned heavy and hers joined it. He moaned over and over, in time with each deep thrust of his cock. She groaned along with him until the room was full of the sound of their pleasure. She tensed her muscles around his cock and his face screwed up. She did it again, holding his cock tight inside her and loving the slight edge of pain brought by each thrust of it into her.

He grabbed her thighs and pounded into her faster, his movements frantic and uncontrolled. She closed her eyes now, lost in the bliss and fire of their coupling. He leaned forwards, lifted her backside off the bed and slammed into her. She threw her head back and moaned, no longer caring if anyone heard her. He grunted and thrust into her again, his cock throbbing and pulsing as he came with a warm rush of seed into her. She locked her feet around him and rode his last few strokes inside her, wanting to cum too.

She frowned when he pulled out of her and then moaned when he pushed two fingers up inside her slick channel and began thrusting while he licked her clit. It was a matter of seconds before the universe exploded before her eyes and she breathed hard as the hot liquid fire of her orgasm swept through her.

A smile crossed her lips as he moved and came to lie beside her. She was surprised but pleased when he drew her to him, forcing her head against his chest. His heart was thundering, outstripping the pace of her own. She closed her eyes and wrapped her arm around him. She wasn't sure what would happen now and she didn't want to think about it. She didn't want to think about how she felt for him or his feelings for her. She just wanted to lay here in silence enjoying the peace and safety of his arms.

Balt took a deep breath and kept hold of Kayla's hand as they walked off the ship into the bright port of his family's palace on Lyra Prime. He made sure she was close to him as they walked towards the main white domed building of the port. His eldest brother had been sent to greet him. He supposed it was better than his parents since he'd neglected to mention he had a guest with him.

More than a guest.

He smiled at the feel of her hand in his and how close behind him she was, using him as a shield from this unfamiliar world. He squeezed her hand and looked over his shoulder at her. When he saw how worried she looked, he stopped and frowned at her.

"There is nothing to fear here." He smiled when she nodded but none of the anxiety in the eyes disappeared. She could nod all she wanted and pretend that she was alright, but he could see straight through her. Her eyes told him everything she really felt.

She glanced back towards the ship and the crew that were unloading it, and then past him towards his brother, Sebastian, where he stood at the end of the gangway, a lone figure in the arched opening of the building.

"He will not harm you... no harm will come to you here. I will not let them touch you." He squeezed her hand again to get her attention. The worry in her eyes melted away enough for him to see that his words had had the desired effect. "Come."

He walked towards his brother, never relinquishing her hand, not even when he stopped in front of him. His brother gave a brief glance at their joined hands and then looked at her.

"We did not expect you to have company," Sebastian said, giving her a curious look.

"This is Kayla. She is the reason I have returned early." Balt looked around him at the empty port. "Are our parents at home?"

"They are always at home," Sebastian said with a smile. Balt nodded in agreement with his brother. His parents rarely left the palace.

His stomach turned with nerves and he swallowed hard. It was the right thing to do for Kayla. His parents would put up a fight about his idea, but in the end they would relent and he would get his way. He always did.

"I must speak with them." He noticed his brother's gaze drift back to Kayla. There was a glimmer of something in his eyes. It was either deep curiosity or surprise. Had his brother figured out why he'd brought her here?

Sebastian's eyes shifted to Kayla's ear and then his own. "A translator? Where is she from?"

He hesitated a moment, unsure how his brother would react to the news that she was a Terran.

Kayla stepped past him, squaring up to his brother with so much confidence that Balt was surprised.

"I have no home... since Lyra destroyed it. I am Terran." Her head cocked to one side, her eyes narrowing on his brother. She released Balt's hand, standing firm and planting her hands on her hips in a show of confidence and defiance.

Sebastian's dark eyebrows rose and he looked at him.

Balt nodded in confirmation. "She is Terran and wears a mark to prove it."

"Marked?" Sebastian said with another curious glance at her. "I do not want to know how it is you came to have her onboard your ship or came to see this mark."

"It's on the back of my neck," Kayla said and Balt cringed when her look turned mischievous. "As for how I came to be onboard his ship... he happened to be given me as a gift from a Sekarian trader on a backwater space port."

Sebastian's eyes widened in horror.

"She's joking," Balt said and Kayla glared at him. "There's a little truth... just... don't tell our parents."

Sebastian shook his head and started laughing. "Whatever you say, little brother."

Balt grabbed Kayla's arm and dragged her along with him as he walked towards the palace. It towered above him, gleaming white and gold in the strong Lyran sun. The rich blue sky above was the perfect backdrop to such a beautiful image as his family's home. The spires around the domes reached towards it, higher and higher, as though they could touch it if they stretched a little more. He walked out of the port building onto the wide balcony in front of the palace and was forced to stop when Kayla did. He looked at her. Her emerald eyes were wide and her mouth was open as she stared up at the palace. Her face reflected all the fascination and awe he felt inside whenever he saw it.

"Come, Kayla," he said and she started walking again. He met his brother's gaze long enough to see the knowing smile in them. Sebastian had figured out his plan. He hoped that Kayla hadn't.

They walked into the building, saluted by the guardsmen at the entrance, and the change in temperature was dramatic. Outside was fiery hot, while in the palace it was cool and dark. He led the way through the winding corridors and across large rooms, heading into the heart of the palace and his parents' day chambers.

When he reached them, he realised that Sebastian had left them. He turned to Kayla and smiled at her.

"Wait here," he whispered, not wanting his parents to hear him and come out. "I shan't be long."

Kayla nodded. His fingers trailed from hers as he left her. She watched him open a large arched wooden double door and disappear inside. The sound of it closing echoed down the long empty corridor. It was cold. She wrapped her arms around herself, nerves fluttering in her stomach like butterflies. Why had Balt brought her here? She wished he'd let her remain on the ship as she'd wanted to. He'd been so insistent on her coming with him.

She looked around at the thick stone walls and the paintings of his ancestors that hung on them, and then noticed some chairs against the wall behind her. She sat down in the middle of the three and hummed to herself while she waited. It was a lullaby that her grandmother had always sung to her. Apparently it had once been the united anthem of her home world. It was a haunting melody now and she wondered if only she remembered it. How many Terrans were left in the universe?

The minutes wore into hours until she lost all track of time. She wondered what Balt was saying to his parents. Whatever it was, it was taking a long time and she was beginning to feel uncomfortable sitting alone in the corridor. Several guards had passed her and given her strange looks.

The door opened and she was instantly on her feet.

"Balt?" she said as he stepped out.

He smiled at her but there was fatigue and worry in his dark eyes. She stepped towards him, tempted to take his hand and offer him comfort, but then thought the better of it. She still wasn't sure how things stood between them. He'd shared her bed more than once in the journey here, but never had he made it clear how he felt. Until he showed her his feelings, she was going to guard hers with her life.

"Come with me," he said in a gentle tone and held his hand out, gesturing towards the open door and the room beyond.

She swallowed her fear and stepped past him into the room. It was expansive and richly decorated in sky blue and gold. She waited for him to close the door before walking any further. She needed him by her. For some reason, he gave her courage and confidence when he was close to her.

He placed his hand against her back and ushered her into the room. She raised her eyes to see a late middle-aged man and woman in front of her. The woman had light brown hair piled up on top of her head, held with shiny gold pins that had cascades of pearls falling from them, and features that said she had been beautiful when she had been younger. Her age showed in the lines of her face though, everywhere except her aquamarine eyes. There was a youthful spark to them. Kayla didn't like the look of it. To her it said that this woman could be ruthless and stubborn. The woman shifted, turning slightly to the side on the couch beside the man, and smoothed the skirt of her long sky blue dress down over her knees.

The man was different. His grey hair was soft and wavy, his eyes dark but kind. He had a nice face, one that said he held compassion and understanding in his heart. His figure was slim, encased in a dark blue jacket and trousers that were a similar colour to Balt's flight suit. He leaned back in the highly decorative couch.

"Mother, father, may I present Kayla." Balt nudged her forward.

She didn't know what to do so she bowed her head.

"She has little breeding." The woman sounded unimpressed. Kayla frowned at her. "I had thought more of the Terrans."

"You must understand, mother, that she has not had an education worthy of her position... she has—"

"Yes, yes... you've said all this," the woman cut Balt off and raked her eyes over Kayla.

She didn't look at all impressed.

"Will you consider my request?" Balt said. "Now that you have seen her?"

"I know we must make amends for what our forefathers did to her people, but you must understand that we cannot simply hand over a planet," the man said.

A planet? She looked at Balt.

"Lyra Five is unpopulated and on the outer rim of our system. The climate is perfect for Terrans and they would be—"

"You have said all this too, son," the man said and then looked at her. A hard look entered his eyes.

She got the feeling that they didn't like the idea of handing over a planet to her people. She looked at Balt, unable to contain her smile when she saw the frustration in his eyes and realised how hard he was fighting for her species. He wanted to make amends for what had happened, to repay the debt. It was so romantic and noble of him. She didn't even think about what she was doing. She just reached out and touched his hand in a light caress. He looked down at it and then at her, right into her eyes.

There was a flicker of something and then he grabbed her hand, bringing her forwards with him.

"Then give the planet to me and I will give it to the Terrans. When I turned thirty, you promised me something..." He sounded nervous now. Kayla could feel his hand shaking in hers. What had his parents promised? "You swore that I could have any gift I wanted... anything... you swore."

The man stood and the woman followed suit. There was shock on their faces.

"We promised you that as a wedding present."

Kayla's heart jumped into her mouth. She looked at Balt. He frowned at his parents.

"It will be a wedding present," he said in a calm and measured voice.

She couldn't believe this. She tried to form words to ask him if he'd gone insane or if he really loved her enough to marry her for the sake of giving her species a new home but they wouldn't come.

"Balt," she whispered, afraid that if she spoke any louder this illusion would shatter.

He turned and looked at her. His other hand claimed hers and he held them tightly. His eyes were full of so much emotion and affection. Perhaps he did love her enough to marry her.

"Kayla... I only have one way of saying this..." He removed the translator from her ear and then his own. She stumbled when he placed his hands around her waist and drew her close to him. Her hands pressed against his chest and she stared into his eyes, too stunned to say anything. "Yoi aishin."

She didn't need a translator to know what those words meant. The horrified gasps of his parents and the tenderness in his eyes and the passion in his voice translated them for her. His kiss confirmed it.

She leaned into it, kissing him with as much ardent desire as he was showing her.

Someone cleared their throat and she broke away from Balt. Her cheeks blazed when she saw his parents were staring. She took the translator with shaking hands and tried to get it back into her ear. Balt smiled and helped her, his fingers brushing her cheek as he trailed them off her.

"I love you, Kayla. Be my wife."

He was insane.

So was she.

She nodded and grinned, barely containing her desire to bounce on her heels. "I love you too."

He kissed her and there was another cough. They broke apart again and both looked at his parents. His mother looked sour. His father sighed.

His sigh became a smile that gave Kayla the impression that he was happy to see his son in love.

"Lyra Five is yours, to rule together."

Kayla stood on the colourful tiled balcony, the warm breeze tousling her hair and the strong sun heating her skin. She listened to the waterfall thundering to the ground almost one hundred feet below her. The hills of this new world, her new Earth, stretched out before her, rising to mountains in the east and lowering to the sea in the west. This was her favourite place to be in all the world. She loved nothing more than to stand here, passing the hours and watching the ships as they came into port in the city below.

Another freighter landed, blowing dust up into the air. It had been six months since the Lyrans had given her species this planet, and people had been arriving every day. The population was growing steadily. Settlements had been given to those who knew how to farm, and the Lyrans were instructing others on how to tend to the land and how to work metal and other materials.

A smaller ship entered the atmosphere and passed the palace. It had been four months since she'd seen that one, and she'd been waiting every day for its return.

She smiled as she heard quick footsteps in the room behind her and sighed when his hands claimed her hips. He always knew where to find her. He stepped up close behind her, moulding her back against his front and placing a kiss on her neck. It felt like eternity since she'd seen him. She closed her eyes and leaned into his kisses, savouring his touch and how good it felt to be in his arms again.

His hands shifted to her stomach and he tensed. She couldn't contain her grin as he turned her in his arms and stared down into her eyes, his own full of one question.

She placed her hands over his where they rested on her swollen belly and he smiled. She'd never seen him look so happy.

"How long?" he said, a tremble in his voice.

"A little over four months. I didn't realise until you were gone."

"Why didn't you send word? I would have come home." He frowned at her now, deadly serious again.

She raised her hand to his face and brushed her fingers across his cheek. "It's far more fun to surprise you with these things. You get so wonderfully serious."

"I do not," he said, his frown intensifying. She moved her fingers up and smoothed the frown away. He smiled. "Perhaps I do... but this is worthy of being serious."

She shrugged and ran her hands over her stomach, staring at it. The first few weeks of knowing she was pregnant had been hard. She'd wanted to break down and tell him, wanting him to come straight back to her and tell her that he loved her like he had that day on Lyra Prime. It was more fun this way though. She did love to surprise him.

"I think this is something to smile about rather than frown," she teased him, a smile still fixed on her lips. She covered his hands again with hers, keeping them against her stomach. "Perfect for Terran-Lyran relations."

He frowned again. "Our child is not an instrument of improving—"

She cut him off with a kiss. It had been too long since she'd seen him and there was far too much talk for her liking. He kissed her a moment and then gently prised her off him.

"Does everyone know?" he said, a little breathless.

She kissed him again, her tongue tangling with his this time. She didn't want to talk about all the formalities of having a baby now that she was truly royalty. She just wanted to stay here in the palace with him and drink her fill of him.

"Kayla." He pushed her off him again. "Do they know?"

She shook her head. "I wanted you to be first... do we have to talk about this right now?"

He looked serious for a moment and then his eyes darkened with hunger. "What would you like to talk about?"

She grinned and pulled him back to her, peppering kisses across his cheek as she spoke. "I don't want to talk at all. I want to kiss you until the sun sets right through to when it rises again."

He reclaimed her lips and she parted them, allowing his tongue to enter and tangle with hers. It felt so good. She'd missed this so much. She'd missed him so much.

She sighed into his mouth and he wrapped his arms around her, holding her close but so gently that she had to smile. He was treating her as though she was breakable. Something told her that he wasn't going to let her out of his sight now, definitely not until the child was born and possibly even beyond that. He would want to stay close, not just because he wanted to share the experience but because of the dangers. She'd had months to think about the things that had happened since meeting him. If the Minervans heard that she was pregnant, they would target her in their attempt to get money from Balt's parents. From now on, they would have to be increasingly careful. If their child were a boy, it would be an heir to the throne.

She leaned back to avoid his next kiss and looked up into his dark eyes. They were full of curiosity when she stared into them for a long time, saying nothing.

"What is it?" he said at last.

She ran her fingers into the shorter hair at the back of his head and smiled up at him. He frowned when she took the translator from his ear. She wanted him to hear this in his own language and from her, not from some device. She removed her own.

"Yoi aishin," she said, a little nervous about speaking his language and getting it wrong.

He was still for a moment, his expression unchanged, and then a smile curved his lips.

"Yoi aishin do... amo tatui sem."

She frowned and put her translator back in before pushing his back into his ear. "Say that last bit again."

"I'm always yours," he whispered against her lips. "It was nice to hear it in my own language. Is there anything else you've learned to say?"

"A few things," she said with a mischievous smile. "My tutor says I am doing well."

"Tutor? You're learning Lyran?" He pulled back, his brows raised high.

"I want to be able to speak to you properly, without this." She tapped the device in her ear. "Lyran is such a beautiful language... I've learned to say so many things."

She removed his translator and her own again, and tossed them into the room, not caring where they landed.

"Kishia wa," she whispered against his mouth.

He did. He pulled her close and kissed her hard, stealing her breath and making her head spin. She hadn't expected him to react so strongly to her speaking his own language. Feeling the urgent need to breathe, she pressed against his shoulders. He released her with a sheepish smile.

She kissed him briefly and then turned in his arms so her back pressed against him and she was facing the outside world. He wrapped his arms around her shoulders and then slipped them under her arms and rested his hands on her belly. She placed hers over them and smiled as she looked out at the panorama.

Now it was truly beautiful. With Balt here with her, it was perfect. Never in all her years had she thought that her life could turn out this way. Never had she thought she could find someone who loved her so much and made her feel as though she was a princess.

He swept the hair from her neck and pressed a kiss to it and then one to her cheek. His breath tickled her ear.

"Aishin... yoi aishin... tatui... tatui... wa naima." He peppered her cheek with kisses and held her close.

She leaned her cheek against his and sighed.

He loved her.

Always.

She smiled as she translated the last two words.

Not a princess.

His queen.

The End

RUNAWAY HEARTS

Heir Prince Lyra I hates his life, and it's only getting worse. Not only do Sebastian's parents force him to remain on Lyra Prime with them and control his life, now they've gone and arranged his marriage. Unable to stand the thought of getting married before he's seen the stars as his three younger brothers do and tasted adventure, he decides to run away. Only that's not as easy as it sounds when you're one of the infamously handsome sons of Lyra.

Terea needs to get away. She's had it with men and her family. When she spots a man who looks as though he has a little money, she sees her chance and pickpockets him. The only trouble is, he's quicker than her. Before she knows what's happening, she's been caught and is agreeing to leave the planet with him. Anything to escape Lyra Prime and her future there.

Terea's plan to escape Sebastian when they've left the planet behind is shattered when he cleans himself up and changes on her, losing his naive air and becoming a confident and dangerously sexy man. A bottle of the strongest alcohol available is her last resort, but getting him drunk to the point of passing out means she'll have to drink too, and before she knows what she's doing, she's sitting astride his lap feeding him the alcohol and kissing him.

When the ship is forced to stop and boarded by Minervan military looking for him, will Sebastian hand himself over to protect Terea? Will Terea stand by and let the man she's falling for get hurt or will she sacrifice herself and return to her family for the sake of saving him? Will two runaway hearts find the freedom they're searching for in each other's arms?

RUNAWAY HEARTS

Heir Prince Lyra I only had one thing to recommend him to women, and it was one thing he wished he didn't have—Royal blood. Never in his life had a woman seen him for who he was. The second they realised he was a son of Lyra and heir to the throne, they changed. Their petty flattery had the opposite effect to what they wanted. It made him leave.

He wished he were like his younger brothers, free of the title of Heir Prince of Lyra. What he wouldn't give to be them, to be enjoying their lives and carving out a reputation for themselves that didn't tie them to the throne. His next two brothers were both captains of the Lyran Imperial Army. His youngest was in training to follow them. He'd wanted to be a captain once, had desired to see the stars and experience the universe's many galaxies.

Leaning against the balcony of his room in the palace, he stared up at the pitch black sky and the millions of glittering stars, longing to be out there with his brothers.

The piece of paper in his hand rustled in the light breeze, reminding him of its presence. Simply put, it was an order. It came from the highest power in the land. It came from his parents.

They had decided it was time for him to marry.

With Balt, the second eldest of he and his brothers, married and settled on Lyra Five with his wife, Kayla, his parents were anxious for another marriage. More particularly, his mother was. He'd got the impression countless times over that his father didn't really care if he or his brothers ever married.

He had to admit that seeing his brother get married had made him consider marriage himself, but he didn't want it to be this way.

He stared at the piece of paper. There was no name on it. She had been written about as though she was a piece of property without any thoughts or feelings of her own. His brother Balt would be furious if he saw this letter. He hated anything that made people out to be a slave or would offend his once-slave wife.

His eyes scanned the page to the proposed date of the wedding. It was only a week away. It turned his stomach so much that he screwed the note up and threw it over his shoulder into his room.

He couldn't marry without knowing the woman first or even knowing her name. It was impossible. He couldn't marry without having seen the universe first. He'd never even been into deep space.

A thought crossed his mind, brilliant and glittering like a jewel at first, but quickly becoming tarnished when his better sense said that his parents would never allow him to go into deep space, not even with his brothers.

He sighed and stared longingly at the stars.

Perhaps there was another way.

The bell rang for dinner and he trudged wearily across his room and out of the door, his thoughts still with the beautiful night sky and his heart still fixed on seeing deep space before he was married. Perhaps the other way was the only way.

He sat down at one end of the long dark wood dining table while his parents sat at the other. Even during his meals he was lonely, left sitting what felt like miles from his parents because that was what propriety dictated. He leaned his right elbow against the table top, propped his chin up on his palm and played distractedly with his food.

"Sebastian!" His mother's voice rang across the room.

His gaze slid to her. She was frowning so hard he couldn't see her eyes. She motioned towards his elbow. He rolled his eyes and sat straight, removing his arm from the table.

At thirty four, he had thought he would have more freedom. His life seemed to be getting more and more controlled the older he got. He was tired of being treated like a child and not like the man he was. His parents never saw the real him. They didn't know him. They only knew the boy they believed him to be—the one they wanted him to be. He sighed again and decided that he would go through with his plan.

He couldn't get married without seeing those stars and another system, or the blackness of deep space. He wanted to see the things his brothers saw and told him about whenever they came home.

"Mother," he said in a cautious voice. "I'm going to visit Balt on Lyra Five."

She snorted. "You certainly are not."

"But the child will be born soon... I would like to be there when it is. I promised Balt that I would be."

"Don't be ridiculous. Kayla will come here to have the child, as tradition dictates."

He frowned. He hated tradition. Why couldn't he have been born the second eldest son? He supposed that the less freedom you had the more you longed for it. Kayla had told him as much once, just after her wedding. She'd been radiant with sheer joy. She'd told him that she'd never felt as free as the day his brother had removed her collar and said she belonged to no one but herself.

He wished he belonged to no one but himself.

He was the property of the imperial family though, and of Lyra. Heir Prince.

"Kayla will not leave Lyra Five. She is intent on having her baby there with Balt and the Terran midwives." He knew that this slip of knowledge would stir trouble, but he didn't care. Right now, he wanted to spite his mother for not letting him leave Lyra Prime and this seemed the perfect way.

"What?" She stood sharply, sending the cutlery rattling when her legs knocked the table. His father placed a hand on her arm. She shook it off. "It was agreed she would come here!"

"Balt says that Kayla said no such thing and that they were going to have the baby on Lyra Five."

His mother stormed towards him. He hadn't seen her this angry since Balt had originally announced his intention to marry Kayla. His brother had guts to go against their mother. Maybe he had the guts too.

He stood, gave her a look that said he was just relating what he'd heard, and then walked away, leaving his parents arguing about where the baby was going to be born.

It would keep them busy for a while. Possibly long enough for him to put his plan into action.

The short walk back to his apartment passed quicker than he'd expected. He locked the door and went to his wardrobes. A rifle through them made it clear that he had nothing to wear that wouldn't make him stand out from the crowd wherever he went. He needed clothing that was a little more common looking if he was going to get off the planet unnoticed.

None of the servants' clothes would do. They were all too recognisable as well.

He took the purse of gold Lynans he kept in his desk drawer and went back to the wardrobe. He stripped off his jacket and his boots, swapping them for a pair of worn riding boots and an old riding jacket. A glance at himself in the mirror made him realise he was even more noticeable now. He growled in frustration, removed the jacket, and went back to the wardrobe. There was just nothing suitable.

At the back of it, he found a moth-eaten cloak that he'd had since forever. His parents had insisted that he throw it away, but he'd always refused. He was glad that he hadn't now. He wrapped it around his shoulders and went back to the mirror. It was better. The old brown cloak would hide his crisp white shirt and tight black trousers. It went perfectly with the scuffed boots. He looked at his face. He had to do something about that. Everyone on Lyra Prime knew what he looked like.

He stared at himself, into his almost jet-black eyes, and ran his fingers over his short black hair. A hat? It was the quickest method of disguise that he could think of. Unfortunately he didn't own any hats.

He was too clean as well. The people using the public freighter transports were likely to look more worn and dirty. He went to his balcony, stuck his hand into the nearest plant pot and rubbed the dirt across his face and neck and into his hands. A look in the full length mirror made him smile. That was better, but he still could be recognised.

A quick ruffle of his hair made him look less like himself. He smiled at his reflection. He actually looked better than he had before. He liked this new hair style. It was wild and rebellious. Exactly how he felt right now.

Deciding nothing else could be done to disguise himself, he went to the balcony and looked over the edge. He made the short drop to the larger balcony below and ran to the steps that led down into the garden. In the far corner, he found the gate he'd stolen the key to years ago but had always been too afraid to use. He unlocked it and walked through. A sense of freedom swept through him when he locked the gate and then turned to face the wide open road that led down into the city.

He was sure there would be a transport leaving tonight. He didn't care which one he got on. He looked at the star-filled sky. He just wanted to be up there.

Running down the road, he kept the cloak closed around him to hide his finer clothes, and tried to remember whereabouts in the city the port was. He stuck to the winding side streets, avoiding the large square at the front of the palace. There would be guards there and he wasn't about to get caught. For the first time in his life, he was going to see how others lived and taste the freedom they did.

He slowed to a walk when the palace began to grow small and distant. His eyes scanned the dark shop windows, running over the displayed goods in fascination. He'd never thought the world would be so colourful and interesting. The shops sold all manner of things, most of which he'd never seen. There were tools in one, material in others, and flowers. He stopped to look at them. He'd never seen such delicate and beautiful blossoms before. They were splendid white irises spotted with rich purple. His eyes fell to the card in front of them. Apparently they came from Lyra Three. Lyra Three was the planet next to Lyra Prime on the sun side. It was hotter there. He wondered if the ship he chose to board would go there. He hoped it would go out of the system and into deep space.

A wide square opened in front of him. Directly across it was a long building with rows of arches along the front and tall arched windows above them. The white roof was a series of domes. A ship appeared from behind it and lumbered into the air, chugging towards an unknown destination. It had to be the port.

He walked towards it and then realised that he'd have to navigate a market in order to reach it. The square was packed with stalls selling goods even more fascinating than those in the shops. It was as though traders that had just landed from distant planets had unpacked their wares and were selling them to anyone interested. He stopped at a few stalls and looked at some of the items on sale. At one of them, he picked up an object that he recognised. He'd seen Acer with something similar last year, but couldn't recall what it was. Acer had only told him that it was something he was fixing for his ship, the Nephis-Lyra. The trader spoke to him, babbling on about prices and trying to get him to haggle for the object. He shook his head and placed it back down.

A group of children ran past him, laughing as they wove through the crowds. He kept a hand over his money, aware that even on a planet as rich as

Lyra Prime, there were still those that needed to pickpocket in order to feed themselves or their families.

The port loomed ahead of him. He slipped through the last of the crowd and out into an empty strip of square. He watched the constant line of people entering and leaving the port. This was it.

He stepped forwards.

Someone bumped into him, almost knocking him to the ground. They fell at his feet with a muffled noise of pain. He looked down to see a small woman kneeling on the hard cobbles. Stooping, he caught her arm and helped her to her feet.

"Are you alright?" Sebastian looked her over.

She wrapped her dark blue cloak around her and nodded. She looked shaken and he got the impression she was scared when she looked over her shoulder towards the market. Was someone following her? He looked there too and then back at her. She was staring at him now. He was glad she didn't seem to recognise him. Perhaps she wasn't from Lyra.

"Are you sure you are alright?" he asked again.

She nodded. "I'm fine... if you'd just release me."

She was speaking Lyran though. Maybe she was from his system. She gave an impatient look to his hand where it gripped her upper arm.

He released it and she hurried off. He looked over his shoulder at the market again and then back at her. He frowned. His eyes widened. His hand flew to his pocket. The money was gone.

By Iskara's wings, she had nerve.

He sprinted after her. The moment she saw he was giving chase, she broke into a run and headed for the port. He had to catch her before she made it into the building. He'd lose her in there.

He increased his speed until he was closing in on her. She looked over her shoulder and gave him a pained look. She slipped on the cobbles just as he lunged for her arm and he fell with her, landing beneath her on the ground. He caught her wrists as she struggled and wriggled, and wrestled with her until she was trapped beneath him.

Terea breathed hard and her face screwed up with effort as she tried to get the man off her. He pressed her wrists into the cold cobbles, trapping them, and frowned at her. There was such darkness in his black eyes. She tried to get her knees free so she could kick him in the balls. He shifted, pinning her legs to the ground with his. Damn it. This wasn't what she needed.

"Let me go." She struggled again. He held her wrists tighter. Her hands hurt and her bones ached. She stilled, fearing he'd break her wrists if she continued to fight him. "I will return your money if you let me go."

"Why did you take it?" he said, his breath sweet and moist against her face. A look of curiosity entered his eyes, chasing away the blackness. He was filthy. From a distance, he'd looked rich and noble. Up close, he looked nothing more than a common beggar. He probably didn't have any money in the purse anyway.

"I need to get off this planet... I only needed a little money."

He visibly swallowed and the pressure on her wrists decreased. He was giving her a funny look. Was it something she'd said? She opened her hand and looked at it, indicating his purse. He snatched it and shoved it into his pocket. He didn't let her go.

She whimpered when he dragged her onto her feet, his hand locked tight around her wrist. No matter how much she tried to prise his fingers off her, he wouldn't let go. She kicked him in the shin. He frowned at her again.

"Why do you need to leave?" The curiosity was still in his eyes. "Is someone after you?"

"It's hard to explain. I just need to get away." She tugged on her arm. He tightened his grip. Her bones ached. He was going to snap her arm if he kept going. She dropped to her knees again, her eyes closed against the pain. He hauled her back onto her feet and towered over her. "Let me go... I won't bother you again."

"Where are you going?"

Damn he was full of questions. She wished she'd never mentioned why she'd been robbing him. Desperate times called for desperate measures. Didn't the people of this planet understand that?

She kicked him again. He cursed in Lyran, voice rich and deep, and then slapped her so hard her head turned to the side. She stood there with her eyes wide and mouth open as she waited for her cheek to stop stinging and her head to stop spinning. She'd never been hit before. She couldn't say that she liked the experience.

"Answer me," he said and she looked at him. It was too dark in the square to see his face properly, but she could hear all the hardness in his voice. He was used to getting answers when he asked a question and she was starting to anger him. He sounded like her father.

"Anywhere," she whispered and her brow furrowed. "Just somewhere away from here."

He went quiet for a moment and then his look changed. All the anger disappeared, leaving a sense of calm behind. She reached out a little with her mind, testing the waters. He was calm, interested. There was a sense of hope and relief about him and something else. Understanding.

"Have you used transport before?" he asked.

She nodded. She'd used it a few times in her life. Getting passage here couldn't be any different to those times. Most space ports worked the same way.

"Then I'll pay for your passage, but on one condition."

"Name it," she said quickly, not wanting him to change his mind.

"I will be coming with you."

She stared at him but before she could say anything, he was dragging her towards the port. He was coming with her? Was this the understanding she'd felt? He wanted to leave this planet too.

He had been heading towards the port when she'd stolen his money.

His hand slid into hers when they entered the port. She looked down at them, frowning at the way he thought he could do as he wanted with her. He couldn't. She tried to get her hand free but his grip tightened and he stopped to look at her.

"If you cannot play along, I will leave you on this planet." He stepped close to her, his voice a silken purr in her ear.

She closed her eyes a moment to savour the strange sensations he'd stirred in her and then opened them again when he stepped away.

The light was better here and she could see him properly. He was handsome. No amount of dirt could hide that from her notice. His almond eyes spoke to her of his feelings, telling her everything he was trying to hide from the world. He did want to leave this planet. She wondered why. A slight frown creased his dark brows and she realised he wanted an answer from her.

"Whatever gets me off this hellish rock," she whispered up at him, her eyes still locked with his.

They narrowed and her gaze fell to his mouth. A smile curved his full sensual lips. She looked away, cursing the blush that burned her cheeks when her thoughts got the better of her. So what if he was handsome. He was rough and a little arrogant too. Those two qualities were enough to make her think the worst of him. As soon as they were onboard the ship, she'd part ways with him and continue with her plan.

He started walking again, his palm pressed into hers and fingers locked tightly against her knuckles. She followed him in silence. The crowd was suffocating and she couldn't see above them. She was too short. She looked up at the man. He was a full head above the people around them. She wondered if the universe looked different from up there. Perhaps it didn't. They were both running away from something after all.

They reached the rows of desks near the barriers that blocked the way to the ships. She noticed the guards and then noticed that the man turned his back to them when he did too. Had he done something wrong on this planet? Perhaps he was a criminal and did have money.

"Where are you going?" he said, close to her. She looked around, hoping a destination would present itself.

"Somewhere out of this system." She tried to remember the route they'd taken to get to it. She scanned the names on the boards above the desks. Each desk had a different destination. She smiled. "Acturus."

He frowned at her. "Acturus?"

She nodded, still beaming. She swore they'd passed through there on their way to this system.

"Acturus is a military base station in space." He released her hand and fixed her with a hard look. "It belongs to the Minervans."

There wasn't just distrust and anger in his eyes, there was fear too. Was it the military factor or the Minervan? She hoped it was the former not the latter and then reminded herself that it didn't matter what he thought. As soon as they were on the ship, she was going to ditch him. A lot of the freighters had women only compartments. She'd hide in one of those and hope that he forgot her.

"It stops at Dliaer before it reaches Acturus." She pointed to the board above the respective desk. "You can alight there. Dliaer is a big port about a day from here. From there you can go anywhere."

He seemed pleased by that. He took hold of her hand again and dragged her towards that desk. She was growing tired of his pulling her around as though she was a ragdoll. Either he had no respect for women or he had little experience of handling them. She glanced at him out of the corner of her eye. He was so handsome that she doubted he had little experience. Women were probably falling over backwards to get his attention. Not her though. She'd had it with men.

She was roused from her thoughts when he shoved his purse into her hands.

"Get us passage." He pushed her forwards. His hand remained against her back the whole time they walked to the desk. She got the impression that he was wary of letting her out of arm's reach with his money.

When she reached the desk and opened the purse, she could see why.

There were at least fifteen gold Lynans in it. She could buy a small ship with this much. She swallowed and her heart jumped when he pressed harder against her back, urging her forwards. For a moment, she'd forgotten he was there. She'd been lost in the fantasy the sight of so much money had given her. With this much, she could run away and set up a shop or something somewhere where her father and family would never find her.

She bartered with the woman behind the desk, ignoring the obscene amount of cleavage her uniform exposed. This world had no breeding. She was glad she'd managed to get away and was one step closer to escaping completely.

She rummaged in the purse for the money when the woman told her the price. The second the woman saw the money, she babbled something about lack of availability and a lot of people travelling to Dliaer. Terea sighed. She should've hidden the money better.

"She says they only have premier passage available." She turned to the man. He didn't seem at all bothered by this news. He just shrugged and waved her back towards the woman, keeping his back to her all the time. Was he scared of the woman recognising him too? She looked at the woman and handed over a single gold Lynan. "Fine."

The woman smiled sweetly and handed her the tickets and the five hundred silver Lynans change. Terea glanced at the man to see if he'd been paying attention and when she realised he hadn't, she pocketed the silver Lynans. She'd need some money for the next part of her trip, wherever that took her.

She touched the man's arm and he took the purse from her and then grabbed her hand. He led the way through the crowd towards the gates into the departures area. When they reached it, she noticed he dropped back and covered part of his face with his cloak. She showed the tickets to the guards and then walked through the gates when they opened. The man followed her.

On the other side, she stopped and looked at her ticket. The ship was in dock five. She followed the signs around the curved arched walkway, looking for the right dock. When they reached it, she stepped through the open archway and her brows rose. If the man hadn't liked the fact it was bound for Acturus, he was going to be even more annoyed when he saw the ship.

Sebastian looked up to see the ship in front of him. It was large. It was dark. It was Minervan.

There was no way he could set foot on that ship. He grabbed the woman by her upper arms and shook her.

"You didn't mention it was a Minervan freighter!" He almost growled the words.

She flinched away, leaving him feeling guilty. He frowned at the ship. He couldn't fly on that. It was too dangerous. It had been bad enough when she'd chosen a ship whose final destination had been a Minervan military port. That had been running a risk. This was just madness. The ship would have Minervans on its crew and Minervan passengers. What if they recognised him?

"It's just a ship... you didn't specify the type!" She jerked out of his arms and glared at him. "Do you have something against Minervans?"

He stared at her. She placed her hands on her hips. Her eyes narrowed into dark slits.

There was something terribly appealing about her when she was angry. It made her dark eyes even darker and her blush lips pouted slightly, drawing his attention to them. A hint of rose touched her pale soft cheeks. Her black eyebrows met in a frown. The irritation radiating from her was alluring. It made him want to argue with her even more, to keep pushing.

A call from the direction of the ship announced that it was preparing to leave.

He looked at the ship. Minervan or not, he had to get on it and get away from Lyra Prime. It was only a matter of time before someone discovered that he was gone. It would be too much of a risk to wait for a different passenger freighter.

The woman was still glaring at him. Perhaps she wanted an answer to her question. She wasn't going to get one. He grabbed her wrist and strode past her. She protested and tried to pull away from him. Turning on her, he used his superior height to look down at her, his own anger rising. She stilled, her eyes wide and laced with fear. He relented when he saw it and loosened his grip so he was no longer hurting her.

"We must leave," he said and she stared at him for a minute, right into his eyes, before nodding.

She'd done that before. He started walking towards the ship with her. Earlier, she'd stared into his eyes like that. It had felt as though she was looking right down into his soul and could see everything there. Afterwards, she'd changed slightly, just as she had this time. Whatever she thought she'd seen in his eyes had made her calm and compliant. He hoped she remained that way until they were on the ship.

The metal gangplank echoed under his heavy footsteps. The sound of hers was lighter, softer. Everything about her seemed soft. He glanced furtively out of the corner of his eye at her. She swept her deep blue cloak over her shoulders with her free hand and then fixed her hair, smoothing the long black locks into place in the elaborate bun at the back of her head. Some of the strands fell back down. His gaze fell to the smooth white column of her throat and her graceful shoulders. She moved slightly in front of him and he openly looked at her now. His eyes followed the sweeping curve of her back to where it narrowed at her waist and blossomed out into full hips that begged to be touched. He swallowed and his jaw muscle twitched when he looked at her long legs. The floor-length rich green dress she wore was slit up the side to reveal her thighs as she walked. He noticed the skin-coloured band around her right thigh. She was carrying a weapon. The thought of that turned him on for some reason. It whispered of danger and adventure, with her.

Something else about her whispered to him. It spoke of the fact she didn't look like a common thief. Her clothes were too fine, her body too well looked after, to be a beggar or pickpocket. She looked as though she was running away from a rich family.

He pushed his cloak over his shoulders as they entered the ship. With such a fine looking woman on his arm, he no longer felt the need to look rough and dirty to fit in. If someone saw them together, they would presume they were man and wife, heading off to some distant planet. No one would associate him with a woman.

A stewardess dressed in a tight black top that covered her to her jaw and tight black trousers took the tickets from the woman. She checked them and then intimated a corridor to her left. The woman followed the stewardess, her hand leaving his. He walked along behind her, eyes scanning the interior of the ship, thankful that she couldn't see him and his fascination. He didn't want her to think he'd never travelled before.

The ship was incredible and far larger than they looked from his balcony as they flew in and out of port. The interior was black and silver, with strips of lights underneath his feet and above his head. The exterior had been sleek but bulky, tapering from the front to a wide flat set of thrusters at the back. He wished that they'd had more time. He would have liked to have walked around the outside of the ship to get a real look at her.

They passed a row of square windows. Opposite them were open rooms crammed with people. This was obviously the deck of the ship where the cheapest seats were. He peered into one of the rooms. People were sitting in groups, drinking and laughing. It looked like fun.

When he turned to continue walking, he came face to face with a man. The man stared at him, black hair and eyes giving him a sinister appearance in the strange half-light. He smiled to reveal sharpened teeth.

Sebastian's heart pounded. He squeezed past the Minervan, keeping his head down, and hurried after the woman and the stewardess. He saw them just before they turned a corner halfway along the corridor. By the time he'd caught up, they were entering a lift. He slid in behind them and smiled briefly.

Too close.

He should have been more cautious. Of course there would be Minervan crew on the ship. The man had been wearing a similar uniform to the female showing them to their seats. His eyes strayed to her as she pressed a button and the lift began to move upwards. Perhaps she was Minervan too.

"This way please," the stewardess said as the doors opened again.

He followed the woman down a long corridor. At the end was the hull of the ship. The windows here were larger, reaching from floor to ceiling. The stewardess turned right before she reached the end of the corridor, leading them down another that was just as wide and elaborately decorated. There was a definite difference between the lower deck and this one. No strip lights lit the hall here. On the walls were beautiful lamps that glowed softly. The floor was carpeted with a silvery cloth. The walls were decorated with silver scroll work that marked a rich contrast against the black metal.

The stewardess stopped in front of a door and swiped their tickets over a circular panel beside it on the wall. The door swished open to reveal a large room. Along the wide rectangular window was a bench seat covered in silver velvet that matched the curtains that hung either side of the glass. He stepped into the room, following the two women, and looked around. There was a smaller room off to his right. It looked like a bathroom. He ignored it and took in the main room. It was bigger than he'd expected. The tickets must have been expensive.

He listened to the woman's conversation with the stewardess while he investigated the large panel on the wall. It was displaying the weather at their destination, as well as current news from across the universe and other information. He was glad that his face wasn't up there. Perhaps his parents hadn't discovered he was gone yet, or maybe they were keeping it quiet for now while the palace guard search for him. Either way, the longer the galaxy didn't know he was missing the better. That way he could travel with more ease and get further out into space.

The stewardess mentioned meals and then went to the door. He frowned when she pressed a button and a black shutter eased across the window. She explained that the shutters had to remain closed until they had left the atmosphere and then bowed before leaving the room.

The door swished shut.

He looked at the woman.

She didn't look happy to be alone with him. He walked towards her and she sat on the bench seat in front of the black window. He watched her long slender fingers work to untie the thick silver ribbons holding her cloak around her neck and was fascinated when she carefully folded it. He swallowed. The front of her dress was rather revealing. The material scooped low to show the curve of her breasts and met in a V in front of them. He tore his eyes away and looked at the display panel. It changed to show information about the ship. He focused there, forcing himself to read it so he wouldn't stare at her. He'd been rude enough to her already without gawping at her like a naive boy.

The ship shuddered and he held his arms out to steady himself.

"What was that?" he said automatically, panic in his voice, and her look said everything.

Now she knew that he'd never been on ship before, at least not one this size.

"The engines." Her soft voice held a smile.

She thought he was green. His eyes fell to her breasts. Desire coiled tight inside him.

By Iskara's wings if she gave him half a chance he'd prove he wasn't.

She patted the seat beside her. "Sit. We'll be taking off soon and the ride can get bumpy when the ship hits full speed."

"Sub-space?"

She laughed at him and looked around the room. "A ship like this, with sub-space? Only a handful of ships have those engines and the capability to use them. This ship would be torn apart."

Now he really did look naive. He should've listened to his brothers more when they'd talked of ships. He should've asked all those questions he'd always wanted to. Silently cursing himself, he sat down beside her and frowned when she leaned across his lap. His eyes widened when he saw right down her top.

"What are you—" He kept the panic from his voice but could do nothing to stop the stirring in his loins.

"Relax. I just thought you might need help getting strapped in." She clicked the safety belt across his waist and then reached over his shoulder.

Her breasts brushed his arm. He closed his eyes and swallowed hard, willing himself not to look at them. He didn't want to find out what she'd do if she caught him staring at her body. Another click and she moved again, away from him. Her arm grazed his neck, sending a shiver down his spine. He breathed deep through his nose to steady himself. The warm flowery scent of her filled his mind, wrapping him up as though her arms were around him, holding him. He tilted his head towards her, wanting more contact. Another click and she stilled.

"I don't know your name," she whispered, incredibly close to his ear. Her breath was soft against his cheek.

He swallowed again, harder this time, and tried to regain control of his senses and his body.

"Sebastian," he whispered back at her and opened his eyes. They met hers. They were as dark as his own, as black as deep space. They sparkled at him and he realised she was smiling.

His eyes lowered to her mouth, to the sensual curve of her satin pink lips.

"Terea." She moved away, leaving him feeling bereft and confused.

She strapped herself in while he fought to clear his head and gather himself. Questions crowded his mind, confusing him further. How had she made him feel so much by doing so little? Her proximity was enough to addle his senses. Her touch drove him out of his mind.

Did she have some kind of power over men? Or was it just him?

He stared down at the straps holding him in, restraining his shoulders and waist. What were these feelings?

There was a lurching sensation, a jolt that made his stomach turn, and then a shudder that shook every bone in his body. He could almost feel the struggle as the engines and thrusters tried to lift the ship out of the dock. The force of them vibrated through him, sending his vision wobbling so much that he had to close his eyes. Everything in the room shook, rattling as loudly as his teeth as they hit against each other. He gritted them.

Surely all take offs couldn't be this rough. If they were, his brothers must have sterner stomachs than his own. If the shuddering continued much longer he was liable to lose what little dinner he'd eaten. He didn't want that. It would perfectly complete the picture of naivety he'd so far painted himself as to the woman. Terea.

He was surprised when she grabbed his hand, her fingers closing tight enough around it that it hurt. Her fingernails dug into his palm. He gritted his teeth against the pain too.

The ship heaved and then a deafening roar filled his ears. He was thrown to the side, into Terea, as the engines kicked in and blasted them towards the atmosphere. Terea's grip on his hand tightened and her other hand joined in. She made a small noise that sounded a lot like fear and he placed his other hand over them, completing the tangle. He held hers tightly, mostly to reassure her but partly to reassure himself too. In all the times he'd watched the ships taking off from the port, it had never looked so difficult. They had always eased up into the air with a chugging noise and drifted effortlessly into space. Perhaps it was just him romanticising what he saw. Maybe all large ships took this much effort to get into the air. From a distance it would be hard to tell.

He opened his eyes when the juddering stopped and the rattling ceased. His stomach continued to turn, flipping over and over. He took deep breaths to settle it and looked at the shutter across the window. Were they through the atmosphere yet? He wished he could see. He wanted to see the stars as his brothers did. He wanted to see the moment they left daylight behind and broke through into eternal night.

Terea's grip on him loosened. He took one of his hands away but kept the other there, allowing her to hold it. He'd never had a woman hold his hand before. It was nice.

Everything felt calm.

He imagined that they were drifting out into space now, effortless and weightless.

A shudder rocked the ship and the sound of the engines increased. Another lurch and he noticed the rise in speed. The whole ship seemed to jolt up and down, lunging all over the place.

"I said it could be rough," Terea said, her face buried against his arm.

They must be reaching full speed as Terea had mentioned. He hoped it didn't stay like this for the whole journey. He'd definitely be sick if it did.

Her hand left his, stealing all the warmth away. She looked at him.

"It won't be long now. It will settle soon and then we can move around again." There was a look in her eyes that he didn't like. Not quite mischief but something close. It gave him the impression that if he let her leave the room, he'd never see her again.

He couldn't let that happen. He needed her to get him passage from Dliaer to wherever his next destination would be. He hadn't paid attention to what she'd said to the woman at the port on Lyra Prime and he didn't want to look like an idiot or wind up in the cargo class area of the ship.

Besides, he was beginning to grow used to her company. He would even go as far as saying he liked having her around.

The ship levelled out and he heard the click of her safety harness. She stood and stretched, reaching her arms out above her head. She looked paler than she had been before takeoff. He probably looked the same. He unclipped the straps holding him in and stood on wobbly legs. He could still feel the ship vibrating if he concentrated hard enough. Either that or he was imagining it.

Terea went to the door. He was about to tell her not to leave when she pressed a button on the panel next to it and the shutters across the window opened, revealing the darkness of space.

He stared out of the window, watching Lyra Prime disappearing into the distance. The sun peeked over the disc of it. It was breathtaking. He sensed Terea come to stand next to him but didn't look at her. He couldn't take his eyes off the scene outside. He could see cloud formations hundreds of miles wide and the crystal blue oceans that lapped golden and green continents. It looked nothing like it had done in the books. It was so much more beautiful.

When it drifted into the distance, becoming too small to be interesting, he looked around to see what else space had to offer. Another planet blurred past and then another. Lyra Five. Its oceans were darker than Lyra Prime's and the land was swathed with deep green. It was stunning.

The next planet passed, this one surrounded by space stations and crowded with ships coming in and out of them. It was Lyra Six. A pleasure planet. His parents had arranged for some of the planet's foremost women to attend to him once for his twenty-first birthday. It had been a night he'd never forget.

His attention drifted across to Terea. Something told him that he'd never forget a night spent with her. It wasn't something he'd been looking for on this trip, but then he'd never expected to find himself with such a beautiful woman. She was watching him and not the world outside. He wondered what she was thinking.

Terea reached out with her mind, touching his lightly enough that he wouldn't notice the intrusion. His mind felt red and warm, full of wicked thoughts that she knew were about her. His eyes told her that. Whatever he was thinking, it was dirty.

Other than his desire, his feelings ran along lines of fascination and contentment, even excitement. She'd already figured out that this was his first time off-planet. For someone who had looked so worldly at first, he was fast beginning to appear sheltered.

She glanced at the door and then back at him. The lust in his eyes had been replaced by intrigue. When she'd gone to the door to open the shutters across the panoramic window, she'd sensed his tension and anxiety. He'd been relieved when she'd returned to him.

He knew she wanted to leave.

Something told her that he'd stop her if she tried to.

She was going to have to find a way to get away from him. He'd served his purpose and, now that she had passage to another system, she had to cut ties with him. She'd had it with men. Her father's bringing her to Lyra Prime when he'd said they were en route to Varka had been the last straw. Now she'd felt the wind of freedom in her hair she didn't want to go back. She never wanted to go back.

"You look as though you need to relax." She smiled sweetly to disarm him. His feelings calmed again. "How about I order a few drinks and then the galaxy will seem even more beautiful?"

He looked out of the window. "It's already beautiful."

He was at that. Her eyes traced the line of his profile—his smooth forehead, straight nose and subtle curve of his lips, down to his defined jaw. The dirt still covered him, but she no longer saw it. She cursed herself for her female weakness and went to the panel on the wall.

Her fingers danced across it, taking her deeper into the menu of food and drink available on the ship. She smiled when she found what she was looking for and didn't hesitate before pressing the image to request it. A few glasses of this and he'd be on his back and she could escape.

She heard him walk across the room and turned her head to see him disappear into the bathroom. The door closed. She thought nothing of it and went to the window. It had been a bumpy takeoff after all. There'd been several moments when she'd been convinced she'd lose what little food she had in her stomach. She frowned and then went back to the panel, selecting some items from the food menu. If she was going to get him to drink then she'd have to drink too. With an empty stomach, she'd be drunk before he was.

Satisfied with her selections, she returned to the window and looked out of it.

He'd said it was beautiful.

She traced patterns in the bright stars, joining them together with her eyes. She couldn't recognise any of the constellations from this angle. They all looked strange and it made her feel cold and alone, as though she had gone to a completely different universe rather than system. She never would've been happy on Lyra Prime. It was too different. The people, the cities, even the air. Even the stars. What had her father been thinking?

The man, Sebastian, stepped out of the bathroom just as she sat down on the long padded seat. His cloak was gone, revealing a crisp white shirt and tight black trousers. Her eyes ran up the length of him, over a body that she could tell was toned beneath his clothes. Whoever he was, he took good care of himself. She'd noticed his hands weren't rough when she'd been holding them. If he worked, it wasn't manual labour. Her gaze reached his face. He'd washed the dirt off and preened his black hair. The short tendrils of it were tangled and pushed back, curling around each other. His eyes bore into hers, dark and alluring. She hadn't thought it possible for him to be more handsome without the dirt, but he was.

The door panel buzzed and a female voice came over it. They were speaking Lyran. She thanked Arkus for the reminder that she was with a Lyran and went to the door. For a moment, she'd been about to speak her native tongue.

She opened the door and smiled, bowing her head in greeting to the stewardess on the other side. The stewardess pushed a large silver floating tray into the room. She pressed a button on the wall and the floor opened to allow a table to rise up. It hovered a foot above the ground, perfectly still, as though it had legs. The stewardess placed the bottle, glasses and food onto the table and then left with the tray.

Terea closed the door and looked at the man. He was staring at the table. He lowered himself onto the long seat in front of the window and stretched his arms out across the back of it, his legs crossing.

His eyes flicked to her.

"I thought we could have a drink... it's a wonderful spirit. It will settle both our stomachs and help the time pass more quickly." She gave him a coy smile, fluttering her lashes a little to lure him in. She felt like adding that she'd been trained well by her family. She knew the best wines and spirits, and how to check the quality of most foods in the galaxy.

He looked over his shoulder, out of the window.

What had happened to the man from earlier? He was different now. There was such confidence about him, such power. His quiet reserve and air made her feel as though she was nothing more than a servant girl, vying for his attention. Why had he changed? The man in front of her now showed no trace of the excitement and fear she'd sensed earlier. She didn't know which she preferred—the confident dashing man, or the naive handsome one.

This one felt more dangerous.

She felt as though she couldn't deceive him, no matter how much alcohol was involved.

She felt attracted to him.

She gathered her scattered feelings and opened the dark blue bottle. She kneeled on the floor while she poured the ruby red liquid into the two small glasses and then rose to her feet with little effort and all the grace of her training. He was watching her. She could sense his interest. He wasn't curious. He wasn't intrigued by the drink. All that interest was directed at her. She sat softly next to him at an angle with her knees close to his. She placed her drink down on the table and offered his to him, holding it by the rim with two fingers and touching the bottom of it with two fingers of her other hand as she presented it.

He stared at it and then at her. She held her smile, extending the drink towards him.

His fingers brushed hers as he took it, sending a shiver through her that she couldn't ignore. She turned away to conceal her blush and picked up her own glass.

Facing him again, she raised her glass and knocked it against his.

"To running away," she said and a flicker of surprise crossed his face and then disappeared again.

It hadn't been hard to figure out. She was running away after all. It was easy to spot someone doing the same.

He eyed the drink, sniffed it as though checking to see whether it was poisoned, and then knocked it back in one go. She watched him closely. He didn't even flinch. She drank hers, letting it ease down her throat and enjoying the hot burning trail that followed it. Her head felt a little lighter.

She picked up the plate of food—small titbits of various meats and pastries. She offered it to him. He declined so she helped herself. It was hard to eat delicately when she was hungry and was trying to get enough food in her stomach to stop the spirit from knocking her out.

Her eyes widened in surprise when he leaned forwards, uncrossed his legs and shifted to the edge of the seat. He refilled their glasses.

"Minervan, I presume. It tastes much like Koji." He held the glass out to her. She went to take it but he moved it out of her reach. His gaze burned her as he raked it over her, from her eyes down to her knees and back again. She swallowed and blinked slowly. He was more universe-wise than she'd given him credit for. He knew it was Koji. "They call it Koji for a reason. Do you know what that reason is?"

She shook her head. She did know, but she wasn't about to make him suspicious by admitting it.

"Koji means death in Minervan. They say it's so strong that it has been the death of men... and women." He offered it to her again, and again moved it out of her reach when she tried to take it. "Come, let me serve it to you in a very Minervan way."

There was a hint of darkness and anger in his voice. She hoped he didn't suspect what she was up to. He shouldn't be so disturbed to find a popular Minervan drink on a Minervan ship, heading to a Minervan space station. She was overreacting.

Before she had time to refuse his offer, his hand was against her back. He ran it up to the back of her neck, tickling it when his fingers cradled her and sending another wave of tingles racing down her spine. She fought the temptation to close her eyes over the warmth and sensuality of his caress, and stared at him. She'd forgotten just how seductive a Minervan way of serving it could be. He held the glass between his index finger and thumb and brought it to her lips. His little finger brushed her jaw line. She closed her eyes now, unable to stop herself. The cold glass touched her lips and she drank the liquid down. It went straight to her head. Her eyes opened when he lowered the glass, tracing it down her neck to her chest, teasing the curve of her breasts. She swallowed hard and stared into his eyes.

He smiled.

Her heart pounded.

Damn him.

She pushed him off her and straightened herself out. "You're a little presumptuous to think you can do that to a woman you don't know."

He knocked back his drink and refilled the glasses. She looked at him. There wasn't even the slightest hint of it affecting him. His feelings were stable—calm and collected. She couldn't detect any change in them. Two glasses of Koji should be enough to start getting him tipsy. Was his stomach made of Varkan steel?

She ate a little more food to bolster her defences against the drink. There was no way she was going to get drunk before him. She had to make it go to his head somehow.

He picked up his glass. She took it from him, making sure that her fingers touched his in the process. He looked at her. She smiled and wet her lips. His gaze fell to them, darkening with desire.

"I know another Minervan way of serving," she said in a calm whisper, gunning for seductive and succeeding. "Would you let me show you?"

He nodded. She knocked her own drink back to give herself a little courage and ignored the hot fire that swept through her veins. She just had to hold it together a little longer and then she could get out of here.

She stood and he raised a brow at her when she handed him the drink. “Hold this a moment.”

His eyes shot to her legs when she hitched the long front panel of her dress up, gradually exposing herself. His gaze followed the hem of her dress as it rose, revealing her shins at first and then her knees and finally her thighs. The visible hunger painted on his face was enough to make her give him a brief flash of her underwear before she regained control and lowered the dress to cover them. She wasn’t supposed to be actually seducing him. This was just about getting away. None of this was real.

His eyes fixed on one spot and his brow rose. He was looking at her thigh. She traced her fingers along the band around it to the small knife it held. His gaze darkened. Did the thought of her carrying a weapon affect him in a sexual way? He looked positively hungry for her now. She undid the buckle and removed the knife and holster from her leg. With a smile, she tossed it onto the table. His attention flicked there for a moment and then focused on her exposed thighs again.

She walked over to stand in front of him, her dress still hitched up. He leaned back when she pressed one knee into the couch beside his thigh. His eyes were wide now, dark but fascinated. Her heart raced, sending her head spinning with the alcohol. Nerves made her tremble. She just wanted to get away. If she fed him the shot this way, the alcohol would go to his head. It had nothing to do with wanting to feel his hands on her, or his lips against hers.

She brought her other knee up, pressed it into the couch beside his other thigh, and held his gaze as she lowered herself to sit on his lap.

He swallowed. She smiled and took the glass from his hand. His hand fell to the couch. She pooled the front part of her dress between her thighs and cocked her head to one side, waiting. He didn’t react as she thought he would. She’d expected his hands to go to her thighs, to touch her. Presented with so much flesh, most men would have reacted that way. Not him though. His eyes didn’t leave hers.

She bit her lip and brought the glass up, taking a sip with half closed eyes. His gaze was intent, powerful. Her head felt light and spun a little. The Koji was getting to her, enough that she didn’t care that she was sitting on his lap in an intimate position about to do the most sensual and seductive thing she’d ever done.

Her tongue poked out, capturing a stray drop of Koji on the rim of the glass. His lips parted.

Leaning towards him, she pressed one hand against his chest and was surprised at the hardness of it. She’d been right. Hidden beneath the shirt was a toned body. A voice at the back of her mind said she’d give anything to see it. She shooed it away and focused on him. He was feeling aroused. Good.

Time to turn up the heat.

She ran her hand up and around his neck, burying her fingers into his dark hair. His eyes narrowed, fire burning brightly in them. She brought the glass to his lips, skimming it across them, lacing them with the Koji. He closed his eyes. Perfect.

Her heart thundered with adrenaline and her eyes zeroed in on his mouth. She denied her own rising desire and ran the glass along his lips again. This time he licked them after she'd made a pass. Her own tongue ran over her lips, mimicking his. She took another sip of the drink and told herself to get on with it and stop teasing him. She wanted to tease him though. She wanted to torture him until he snapped and some primal instinct inside him took over.

She shifted on his lap and his jaw muscles tensed. He liked that. She glanced at his hands. She moved again and his fingers flexed and inched closer to her thighs.

She brought the glass to his lips. He parted them and she tilted the glass, slowly tipping the liquid into his mouth. He frowned. His hands went to her thighs, sending a jolt through her that electrified every nerve ending in her body and made her groin throb. He slid them higher. She pressed her cheek against his, trying to steel herself against the effect he was having on her. Her fingers tipped the glass up and then it fell from them, tumbling to the floor as his hands reached her backside and pulled her closer.

She breathed hard into his ear, struggling for control, and dragged her cheek against his as she drew back. Her eyes met his for a moment, long enough to see all the desire and sense it in him, and then she closed hers. Her hands captured his cheeks. She kissed him.

It wasn't gentle or sweet. It was rough, demanding and passionate, and she couldn't stop herself. Her mind screamed that she was supposed to be escaping now, that the Koji had done its work and he was beyond tipsy. Her heart screamed that she had to stay right here, where it felt so good and warm, and where she felt so safe. Her body cried out for his touch.

She leaned forwards, pressing him into the back of the long seat and pinning him there with her hands. They pushed against his shoulders, restraining him. His hands caressed her thighs, stirring the fire inside her until she felt a slave to her desire. Her teeth clashed with his as she kissed him, their tongues tangling and breath hard against each other's lips. She didn't care. She needed more. He tasted sweet like Koji but he felt strong. His fingers flexed against her backside, drawing her closer still. He raised his hips and ground against her, eliciting a moan from her that she didn't even try to contain.

Her hips moved against him, her heart pounding when she felt the evidence of his arousal rubbing her crotch. She kissed him harder, lost in the hunger and the feel of him.

This wasn't supposed to have happened.

She pushed off him but his hands went to her back, stopping her from escaping.

She stared into his eyes. This wasn't right. She'd had it with men. They were nothing but trouble. She had to get away.

His hands locked against her, holding her tight. She frowned at him, pushed against his chest and then pleaded him with her eyes to let her go.

"Stay," he whispered and she stilled in his arms. There was such an earnest look in his eyes and no trace of lust in his feelings. He wanted her but it wasn't empty desire feeding his hunger. She touched his cheek, trying to decipher his feelings and needing the contact to make them clearer. "I can protect you... whatever it is that you're running from, we can run together."

They were tempting words, an alluring promise that spoke to her heart and provoked a response. It told her to stay. He was strong. Perhaps he could protect her.

But he was Lyran.

She turned her head away from him, needing to see something other than his face in order to make her decision. He was too tempting, too handsome and powerful. She closed her eyes. Could he really protect her? Could anyone?

She grabbed the bottle and swigged it, needing the numbing affect to kill off the part of her brain telling her that she was insane. He took the bottle from her and she opened her eyes. He drank some and then leaned towards her. She breathed in sharply when his tongue brushed her neck and he kissed it. It sent tingles racing across her skin. Her eyes closed again and she tilted her head back. His free hand tightened against her upper back, supporting her as he kissed across her chest.

Her hand found his and she took the bottle again. She drank another mouthful and then reached out behind her and placed it down on the table.

Even if he couldn't protect her, she still wanted this time with him.

His mouth reached her breasts and he made fast work of the laces holding her dress closed. She stared at the ceiling with a wide open mouth as he exposed her to the cool air of the room. His fingers grazed her nipple as he pulled the material away and then she moaned when his lips fastened around it. She arched into him, her hand settling against the back of his head while her other one went to his shirt. She wanted it off him. She wanted to see him and feel him.

She unbuttoned his shirt and pushed the two sides apart, exposing his body. It was a struggle to get him off her, but she shoved him until he gave up and leaned back into the seat. Her eyes raked over his body. It was stunning. Golden smooth skin stretched tight over pronounced muscles that made her mouth water and her pussy throb.

She didn't care if he was Lyran or a criminal or that she didn't know him. This attraction was too strong to ignore. She had to have him. It would ruin her, but it didn't matter. Perhaps if she was tainted by another man, her father wouldn't be able to give her to the highest bidder. Perhaps no one but this man would want her then.

She'd be happy if that were the case.

Her fingers traced down his chest to his stomach and from there to his trousers. She unbuckled them, ignoring his weak protests, and slid her hand inside to find his hard cock. It was bigger than she'd imagined it would be. The skin was silken and hot. She kept one hand against his chest as she wriggled out of her underwear, having to shift onto one foot at a time to get them off. It was a farce and she was thankful he didn't laugh at how ridiculous she must have looked. His eyes never left her face.

When she was free of her underwear, she tugged his trousers down enough to release his cock. It rested flat against his belly. She met his gaze and ran her fingers down the length of it. His eyes darkened and narrowed. She smiled, swallowed her nerves, and stroked it again. This time his eyes rolled closed and he sighed.

She'd been taught well about how to pleasure a man but all that knowledge was rapidly leaving her as she sat astride his legs, treading the fine line between going forwards and running away. If she did this, she would spoil herself. No man would want her. Her father would kill her.

If she did this, she would be a woman and she would be happy that her first time hadn't been with a man she had been given to.

He was a man of her own choosing.

He opened his eyes as she took hold of his length, wrapping her fingers around it. His lips parted as though he was going to say something and fear lanced through her when she sensed he was going to tell her to stop. She kissed him, silencing his words and distracting him. He couldn't stop her. She didn't want to stop.

His hands wrapped around her back, tight and strong, as she raised herself up and moved forwards. Nerves fluttered in her stomach when lowered herself and the tip of his cock pressed against her slick arousal. She kept going, driven by desire and a need to escape her old life completely.

Their sighs combined when she bore down on him, his cock sliding into her. It stung but she didn't let it show. She didn't want him to know that this was her first time. She'd been told everything, shown everything. She knew what to do.

He stopped kissing her and pushed her backwards, his eyes searching hers. She kept the answer to their question hidden inside. He didn't need to know. Closing her eyes to hide from him, she grasped hold of his shoulders and raised herself up the length of his cock. She moaned at the delicious friction and then eased back down. It felt so good. Her teacher had never told her how good it was.

She moved again, slowly building a rhythm that had him breathing hard and her heart thundering. He grabbed her hips, assisting her, and slid further down the chair. Her pussy hit his pelvis on the way down and she groaned at the sweep of pleasure that spread from her clit.

Her eyes opened and she stared into his, losing herself in him and the feeling of their joined bodies. It was divine. His breath was hot against her skin, washing over her, his fingers grasping her waist. He tensed beneath her and she moaned hoarsely when he bucked up inside her, hard and rough. She moved faster, sliding up and down his cock, riding it into oblivion. He dragged her back to him and kissed her so deep that she lost all sense of who she was and who he was. They became one inside her, one mind and one heart, one soul and set of feelings. She clung to him, moaning into his mouth with each thrust of his cock into her. Her whole body tightened.

So did his.

He groaned against her lips, deep and strained, as he came, shooting his seed deep into her. She pressed her cheek against his and kept going, reaching for her own orgasm.

It came swift and fast, rushing through her like molten lava and leaving her breathless. Bright white sparks burst against the darkness of her closed eyes. She buried her face into his neck and stilled, keeping him inside her and breathing hard against him as she trembled.

That definitely wasn't like her teacher had told her it would be.

His arms wrapped around her, holding her close. She nuzzled his neck and leaned hard against him, sagging in his embrace and memorising how comfortable she felt.

Sebastian stroked her hair, his fingers loosening it from the bun at the back of her head and combing through the long dark length of it. Her breath was hot against his throat but was becoming steady. He knew she'd never admit that she was a virgin, and she hadn't acted like one. She'd been incredibly skilled and confident for one without any real knowledge of what she'd been doing. He held her closer, a need to protect her rising up inside him, and kissed her exposed shoulder. Her breasts pressed against his chest, warm and soft.

He hadn't expected this to happen with her, and he got the impression neither had she. She'd ordered the strongest drink on the menu in the hope of getting him drunk, that much was obvious. What she didn't know what that he'd had plenty of experience of drinking with soldiers, with his brothers all being in the imperial army, and he had drunk them under the table every time. A third of a bottle of Koji was never going to be enough to make him pass out. He could probably manage a whole one before that happened.

She shifted but he held her, forcing her to remain. His soft cock slipped from her warm folds and he wished he were back inside her. When he'd been in her, an incredible sensation of completion had filled him. He'd felt so connected to her. It was probably an illusion brought about by the alcohol.

He frowned when a strange feeling rose up inside him.

"We're slowing down." She pulled back, looking out of the window behind him.

He stared at her a moment, taking in her beautiful flushed cheeks and bright eyes, and then looked out the window too.

They were in deep space. They must have left the Lyra system behind while they'd been making love.

An alarm sounded, low and booming, loud enough that Terea covered her ears.

"What is it?" she shouted over the noise.

He could see fear in her eyes when she looked at him for an answer. He lifted her off him, tucked himself back into his trousers and did his shirt up.

"Wait here." He touched her cheek to reassure her and went to leave.

She caught his hand. "Where are you going?"

"I'm going to see what's happening. I won't be long. Just stay here and don't let anyone in." He smiled at her, hoping it would help calm her nerves. She shook her head.

"I'm coming with you." She went to stand. He placed a hand on her shoulder, forcing her to sit back down.

"I'll be right back. You'll be safe here."

He left before she had a chance to protest again. The door closed behind him. His head spun and he pressed a hand to it. Perhaps trying to take command of a situation with a sex and Koji addled brain wasn't the brightest of ideas. He cleared his throat and walked down the corridor. It had to be done. He needed to know what was happening.

The ship rocked and he grabbed the wall as he was thrown to one side. He waited for the vessel to steady and then continued walking down the corridor. At the end of it, he turned right and went to the window. His heart accelerated when he saw the Minervan fighter docked with the ship.

What did the military want with a transport ship?

He left the window and headed for the lift. The moment he neared it, the doors slid open and he ground to a halt.

"Cruskin!" he said under his breath and stared at the five men.

They shouldered their weapons.

He raised his hands.

This really wasn't good.

One of the men stepped forwards, his sharp teeth glinting in the low light as he grinned. The other four flanked him with their large black laser rifles trained on him.

He frowned and gritted his teeth as the man grabbed his hands and twisted his arms behind his back. Who had sent them? Lyran military had no right to board a Minervan vessel. Was that the reason the Minervans had boarded the ship, or were they acting for their own system?

He closed his eyes and winced when they locked thick metal cuffs around his forearms, pinning them behind his back.

"What's happening here!" A female voice echoed down the corridor.

He looked up.

Terea.

Stupid woman. She'd get herself killed.

She stormed towards them and he noticed that she'd dressed but hadn't put her cloak on. A glance at the man holding him revealed that she had the Minervan's attention.

"This man is—" The man started.

"This man belongs to me." She cut him off. Sebastian raised a brow. He belonged to her? She gave him a little look that made him even more confused. It looked as though she was asking him to keep quiet and play along. She was the one who was better off keeping out of this. He'd told her to stay in the room for a reason. He didn't want her getting hurt.

"We have orders to detain him in the name of Minerva."

"Who's orders?" She stepped up to the man. She was fearless.

Sebastian tried to look at her but the man turned him away so all he could see was a wall and the two guns of the men nearest him. They were very close to his face.

"Chief General Misea's," the man said and then added, "and King Atelier's."

Silence.

Sebastian tried to move so he could see what was happening but the soldier nearest him pushed the rifle in his face in an obvious warning to keep still.

"I'll repeat myself just this once," Terea said and he heard her move. "This man belongs to me. No harm will befall him. I will tell your Chief General in person. Take me to him."

She was asking a lot. He frowned at the wall and then the gun, waiting for their reaction to what she'd said.

"Certainly, my lady," the man said and the soldiers nearest him lowered their guns.

My lady?

Why was a woman of rank running away? If she had the power to make these men release him and go against their orders, then she had to be important. He risked it and turned to face her and the man. The man bowed his head to her and then reached around and pressed the button on the tight metal cuffs that had been restraining Sebastian's arms. They clattered to the floor.

"If you would accompany us," the man said to Terea and indicated the lift.

"May I have one moment?" she said and the man nodded. She turned to face him.

Her fingers brushed his cheek and he stared at her.

"I don't know what you've done wrong," she whispered with tears in her eyes, "and I don't need to know. I think this is goodbye."

He frowned. "Goodbye?"

"If I go with them, I won't be coming back. I'll see to it that they don't follow you. Get away from here. I hadn't realised Minervans wanted you. If you'd explained that to me..." She placed her palm against his cheek and the tears in her eyes trembled on the brink of falling. "All this could have been so different. We could've been free."

Her hand slipped from his cheek to rest on his chest for a moment before it fell to her side. He stared at the space where she'd been when she turned away and started walking towards the lift and the man.

"Wait!" He took a step in her direction.

She stopped and turned her head to the side, but didn't move to face him completely.

"Don't follow me," she said in a pained voice. A tear streaked her soft cheek. "They'll kill you if you do... and I don't want that. I'd rather live a life knowing you were out there somewhere and we could meet again, than spend it mourning you."

He reached a hand out to her but she walked away. She stepped into the lift and turned to face him, her head bent and eyes fixed on the floor. As the doors slid shut, she looked up at him and smiled.

This wasn't right.

In Iskara's name, what was she thinking, handing herself over to the Minervans and bargaining for his life. Without him there to protect her, they might harm her, or worse. Her words rang in his head, a veiled declaration of feelings that made him warm inside but caused his heart to ache. A few hours with her had been more wonderful and adventurous than his entire life. He wanted her back. He couldn't leave her to disappear. What if he never saw her again?

He stood in the hall staring at the wall and not knowing what to do. If he went after her, he'd be going against her wishes and placing himself in danger. He knew the Minervans wouldn't kill him, but they would ransom him, and they might hurt her in order to make him speak and tell them the secrets of Lyra. It was impossible for him to choose between her and his people. He wanted to protect them both.

But he had to protect her foremost.

He ran back to the room, grabbed the knife she'd tossed onto the table, and then back out again.

He sprinted to the lift and pressed the button. The doors opened and he scanned the deck listing on the panel until he found the docking bay. He hit the button for it and paced the small cylindrical room while it went down. The doors slid open to reveal the cargo hold of the ship. A light caught his attention and he frowned when he realised it was doors closing.

"Terea," he whispered and ran towards it.

Before he could reach it, the doors had shut completely and then the ship rocked as the Minervan fighter disengaged. He braced himself against the shaking and stared at the closed airlock. His heart sank. She was gone.

He walked slowly to the door and stared through the small glass window and the window on the other door in the hull. The Minervan fighter drifted backwards, turned and then disappeared from view. He leaned forwards and pressed his forehead against the glass.

His eyes lost focus as he placed his hands against the cold metal door.

Emptiness filled him.

He'd never see her again.

The ship shook again but this time he didn't care. It was probably another Minervan ship come to take him in anyway. How had they found him so quickly? Had one of the crew recognised him?

"Your Highness."

He frowned and looked to the side without moving. There were several men stood there, all wearing the Lyran Imperial Army flight suits. He heaved a sigh and pushed away from the door when they stepped aside and his brother, Acer, walked towards him.

"You gave us quite the scare, what with that Minervan fighter. Good thing for you we showed up when we did and they high-tailed it." Acer smirked and slapped him on the shoulder. "Sorry, old man, I've got orders to bring you home."

"I need to go after them." Sebastian pushed his brother's hand off him and frowned. "I never ask you for much, but I need you to do this for me. You will do this for me as my brother."

Acer looked shocked for a moment.

"I can't go against orders issued by my superiors, you know that. What you're asking me to do is impossible and would most likely result in destruction of either of the ships or war." Acer's look turned dark and serious.

Sebastian realised that he was right. All was lost whatever he did. If they went after the Minervans, they would open fire and Terea could be injured or killed in the battle. That battle could lead to war between the Lyra and Minerva. The relationship between the two systems were strained at best, and it would only take a single push to break the tie between them completely and push them into war. He couldn't put the lives of his people at risk for the sake of her, and he couldn't risk her. He had to do as she'd asked and go on without her, hoping one day that they'd meet again.

He lowered his head and sighed in resignation.

"Besides, I don't have time to be running after Minervans. I have strict orders to get you back in time for your wedding. I hope you enjoyed your jaunt, brother, because when you get back, you're going to be under lock and key."

Acer's words chilled him to the bone. He'd forgotten that returning to Lyra Prime meant returning to be married. He knew his parents and they weren't going to let him out of their sight until he was wed. There was no way he'd be able to escape again and find Terea.

"Come." Acer placed his arm around his shoulders, grinning. "The whole of the galaxy is waiting to see you get hitched."

Sebastian couldn't manage a smile or anything remotely near one. He stared out of the airlock windows at the dark space beyond. He'd seen the stars as he'd wanted but at the same time, he'd found so much more. He'd found the woman he wanted.

Now he'd never see her again.

Sebastian stared through the tall glass panelled doors that led onto his balcony, feeling nothing and seeing nothing. It was a matter of minutes now. This week had been the longest and most painful of his life. His parents wouldn't hear a word of his protests and had banned the mention of Terea's name. They'd assured him that he'd forget her.

What did they know?

It had been a week and he hadn't stopped thinking about her, replaying every moment in their short time together. He'd never forget her. He'd never stop thinking about her.

Acer had been little comfort, and neither had Balt. Not even his youngest brother Remi had been able to lift his spirits. He'd banned them all from his room two days ago. He couldn't bear to speak to anyone anymore. He only wanted to see her and speak to her.

The only one who had managed to get a smile out of him had been Kayla, and that was because she'd reassured him that he would see Terea again one day and that he could divorce his future bride once his parents were dead and he was king. It had even made him laugh for a moment. She knew his family's stubbornness so well and she'd only been with them a short while.

"Your Highness, it's time," someone said as they opened the door to his room and then left again.

He stood and sighed as he walked to the door and followed them down the hall. Kayla was right. In a few years, his parents might be dead and he could divorce his current wife and find Terea again. He hated to wish that fate upon them, but he couldn't help himself. He longed to see her.

The sun was bright today, warm on his face as he stepped out of the palace and onto the white wide open square in front of it. The walk to the end of the rich blue line of carpet that marked the aisle was long and made him even wearier. His heart was heavy, empty. He wondered if it would always feel this way, as though it was missing and a black hole had opened up in its space, sucking every feeling into it and leaving him numb.

The priest said something to him that he didn't bother listening to. He stood with his back to everyone, the gathered hundreds that sat either side of the aisle, and stared off into the distance.

The fanfare began. He didn't turn around. He didn't care if it was tradition to watch the bride approach. It would give him no joy to see her. He wanted Terea. His eyes went skyward and he wished he were out there amongst the stars with her, free of this life. She'd wanted to be free with him. She'd said as much. Had their short time together affected her as deeply as it had affected him?

The woman came to a halt beside him, dressed in black and silver. He glared at her where she stood facing the priest, her side to him and her face hidden beneath the black veil.

A Minervan?

His lip curled in disgust.

His parents were marrying him off to a Minervan?

The fanfare ended and the priest called for everyone to stand. Sebastian turned to face her. She lowered her head, her hand disappearing under her veil. He frowned as she pressed the back of her index finger to below her eyes as though she was catching tears. Was she happy or sad? The priest told her to turn to face him. She turned her head away instead and took a long deep breath as though trying to control her emotions. The priest again told her to face him.

She did this time.

She turned with head bowed and stood in silence as her attendants lifted her veil and placed it over her hair.

He frowned and stepped back.

Impossible.

She raised her head slowly, her expression sad until her eyes reached his face. Her frown matched his.

"You're the Lyran I was running away from?" Terea said, too shocked to take any notice of the priest or the audience they had.

It was impossible.

Was she dreaming?

He hesitated a moment, his mouth hanging open and his feelings in disarray, telling her that he was having difficulty understanding this too.

She smiled and he followed suit.

"Heir Prince Sebastian Lyra I." He held his hand out to her as though introducing himself.

She placed hers into it and realised he was shaking as badly as she was. "Princess Terea Atelier."

She laughed when his fingers closed around hers and he raised her hand to his mouth and kissed the back of it.

"I can't believe I ran away from you." She frowned at him. "Were you running away from me too?"

He nodded and gave a low laugh. "What a pair we are."

She stepped up to him and ran her free hand up his dark blue jacket, curling it around his neck. "We certainly are."

Her eyes rolled closed when he dipped his head and kissed her, his other hand wrapping around her back and tugging her close until her body was pressed against his.

"Your Highness, it isn't supposed to start with a kiss," the priest whispered.

She smiled when Sebastian looked at him and then at her. "It always starts with a kiss."

"Your Highness, I implore you."

She pressed her hand against Sebastian's chest to stop him when he leaned towards her. The priest thanked her with a smile. It was painful stopping Sebastian when all she wanted to do was kiss him. She held his gaze while the priest continued with the ceremony. Sebastian looked so handsome, his black hair tousled by her fingers and his tight blue jacket emphasising the broadness of his chest and shoulders. She shook her head.

"To think, I thought you a common thief," she whispered, hoping not to disturb the priest. She couldn't stand here mute when she had so many things to say to Sebastian. She'd thought she'd never see him again. This past week without him had been hell. She'd thought of only him, had cried her heart out every day until she had run out of tears.

He smiled, his dark eyes shining with it. Tears rose into hers, but this time they were tears of happiness. She couldn't believe she'd run away from her arranged marriage only to end up in the arms of her future husband anyway. At least this way she felt as though he was someone of her own choosing. She would have to thank her father now. He'd been furious when she'd been brought back and had refused to marry the Lyran prince.

She was so thankful that her father was stubborn. She might have talked her way out of marrying Sebastian.

The backs of his fingers brushed her cheek. "And I know you're a thief."

She dropped her gaze to her feet, unable to look him in the eye. "I admit, I did steal five hundred silver Lynans from you."

His hand opened and cupped her cheek. He raised it, forcing her to lift her head and look at him again.

"You stole more than that," he whispered.

She frowned. "I did?"

"You stole my heart," he said with so much affection in his eyes that she blushed.

Before she could open her mouth to respond, he was kissing her again. She closed her eyes and leaned into him, her arms going around his neck. The kiss was sweet and gentle, filled with love and tenderness that made her melt inside. She tightened her hands against him, not wanting to let him go.

The priest cleared his throat. This time they both ignored him.

He sighed and then said, with a slam of his book, "I pronounce you husband and wife."

She smiled against Sebastian's lips when he grabbed her around the waist and kissed her hard.

Her eyes widened when his hands slid lower and he scooped her up into his arms, cradling her with one arm against her back and one hooked under her knees. He didn't stop kissing her as he carried her down the aisle. A murmur rose amongst the gathered guests. She could sense their curiosity and their intrigued stares.

"Where do you think you're going?" A strong female voice cut through the rest.

Sebastian stopped and his lips left hers. She craned her neck to see one woman standing and recognised who it was. His mother. Sebastian's grip on her tightened.

"This is Terea." He smiled wide. "I suppose I can mention her name in our house again now that she's my wife?"

His mother looked shocked.

"For once, I am glad that you are as stubborn as a Gavaelian farnsk." His smile became a grin and he started walking again.

Terea looked up at him, at her husband, and wondered just what gods of the universe were smiling on them to bring them together like this. Perhaps Iskara and Arkus were working together for once.

"Answer me, young man!" His mother's voice rang in the distance.

He didn't.

She looked at the people they were passing as he walked down the aisle with her and then towards the palace they were heading towards.

"Where are we going?" she said with a curious frown.

He lowered his head and kissed her cheek before drawing back and looking deep into her eyes.

"To catch up... I have a bottle of Koji in my room." He grinned. It was infectious. She couldn't help smiling at him as she remembered their night together.

"We have a lot of catching up to do." She pulled herself up so she could kiss him.

He didn't stop walking. She peppered his cheek and neck with kisses.

"You don't care that I'm Minervan?" She reached out to his mind a little, wanting to see if he told her the truth.

"Not at all." He started up the steps to the palace with her. It was cooler inside the building. She leaned back and looked at him. He wasn't lying. He really didn't care. "But if you keep invading my mind..."

Her eyes widened.

"You can feel me?"

He nodded. "It only happened after we'd—well, you know what happened. I was so addled with our feelings and the Koji that I didn't realise until after... and I didn't know that it was a Minervan gift."

"It isn't." She played with the hair at the back of his head. "My mother was Varkan. It's a trait I picked up from her. No one knows I have it."

"No one but me," he corrected.

"I still can't believe I was running away from you, and ran right into your arms."

He pressed his cheek against hers and squeezed her.

"And here you'll stay, my love," he whispered into her ear.

She sighed and buried her face against his neck, relieved that she had found him again and that his feelings for her were the same as her own.

"My love," she echoed and closed her eyes.

He pressed a kiss to her hair.

"I like feeling you happy." He turned down a corridor.

She smiled.

"I'll never be sad when we're together," she whispered.

He held her tighter and she felt warm inside when she sensed all his love for her and his need to protect her. She'd never felt so happy.

He was happy too.

"If that's the case," he whispered back at her. "I'll never let you out of my arms again."

She'd like that.

She would stay in his arms.

Forever.

The End

FIGHT FOR LOVE

Lieutenant Lyra IV is as sinfully handsome and irresistible as his elder brothers, but the one woman he wants seems to be immune to his charm. Every man in his squadron is falling over themselves to win her. Literally. When the reward is getting to see her, not even he can stop himself from getting hurt in training every day. Losing feels like winning when he ends up on her inspection table, and the pain means nothing when she touches him.

Nurse Emmanuelle knows exactly what the devilishly tempting and handsome Lieutenant Lyra IV is doing and she's not going to fall for it or his attempts to make her call him by his first name, Remi. It's her duty to keep her distance and maintain a professional relationship with him, even if her heart and body is crying out for more.

When the fleet is called back to Varka Two where Remi almost lost his life, he can't waste any more time. This time, he might not make it back. A kiss that sets both their hearts on fire leads to more than he'd dreamed of, and makes both their feelings clear, but will it be too late?

Facing overwhelming odds, is Remi strong enough to survive the battle and return to Emmanuelle? If he ends up on her table again will Emmanuelle be able to save the man she loves? Will they win their fight for love?

FIGHT FOR LOVE

"Lieutenant Lyra IV, you're really going to have to start being more careful in combat training. This is the third time you've been in this week." Nurse Emmanuelle, the most beautiful nurse in the entire fleet, leaned over him.

She motioned for him to move his hands out of the way. Remi did. He reached them out above his head and grabbed the end of the inspection table he was laying on. He flexed the muscles of his bare torso and arms for her. She didn't seem impressed. Her fingers pressed against the mottled bruising on his right side, her touch so light he barely felt it.

His gaze strayed back to her face. She was beautiful when she concentrated like this, intent on her work, her fine silvery eyebrows knitted together. She turned, flicked her long silver hair from her face, and sighed as she picked up one of the tools from the black tray table beside him. His gaze slid to her body and the tight dark blue dress she wore. They shifted across to the buttoned front of it and then rose to her face again when he reined his desire in.

"I can't help it." Remi continued to study her face, watching her tongue wet her delicate rose lips as she turned on the device she held. He'd never figured out where she was from. Perhaps she was an angel of Iskara. She looked like an angel. "They're all stronger and faster than me."

She shook her head a fraction, a smile curving those delicious lips. "I find that very hard to believe."

He smiled at her when she looked at him, her grey eyes touching his a moment before she went back to her work.

With a nurse such as her posted to his squadron, was it any surprise all the men kept getting hurt? He could handle any man here in a one on one fight, but when the reward for defeat was getting to see her, he didn't have the heart to win.

She held the device two inches from his skin and ran the red band of light over it. He held the flinch inside as it hurt, stinging as his body was repaired. It was still worth it, even though it hurt more than getting beaten up in the first place.

"There, all done. You can put your shirt back on now, Lieutenant Lyra IV." She placed the device back down on the tray and stepped back.

He swung his legs around over the side of the black padded table and pressed his palms into the edge of it as he sat and looked at her.

"Why won't you call me by my real name?" Her constant use of his title irritated him. She called others by their name. Everyone but him. "Call me Remi."

She shook her head. "You know I can't. I don't make the rules."

"But you can break them." Remi reached out to her with his left hand and winced when his shoulder grated. His other hand went to it, holding it tight. He must have damaged it during the fight.

"Is it bothering you?" Emmanuelle said, her voice low and concerned.

He nodded. "All the time."

"Not the name thing." Her tone caught a note of impatience and then softened again. "Your arm."

He looked at it when she touched it, as light and gentle as usual.

When he was in his uniform, he could easily forget that it wasn't really a part of him, at least in the sense that he hadn't been born with it. He'd been given it two years ago after he'd lost his arm in an insurgence on Varka Two. It had been his first mission. It had gone horribly wrong. The Varkan's had been waiting for them. Half of his squadron had been killed. He'd been lucky to only lose an arm.

The fleet doctors had done their best, replacing his arm with a fully cybernetic one. It had taken them a whole day of surgery to attach all the nerve endings to the sensors in the arm. He flexed his fingers. When he thought hard enough, he could almost feel the metal joints moving beneath the dark silvery rubber skin. The nurses and doctors had told him it was nothing to be concerned about. It was purely a residual memory of his old arm he was feeling, and not the workings of his new one. He wasn't convinced.

Emmanuelle's fingers traced over the elastic rubber skin covering the metal bones of his arm. He felt every sweep and press of her touch, as real as it would have been if she'd touched his other arm.

"How does this feel?" She raised his arm up and moving it around to different positions.

Remi's shoulder grated again when she pushed his arm out to the side and brought his wrist towards his chest.

He winced.

She lowered his arm and disappeared behind him. His eyes closed when she touched his back, her hands warm against him. Her fingers pressed into his shoulder blade.

"I don't think it's your arm," she breathed close to his ear.

He sighed and then got the better of himself. "So what is it?"

"Just the Lyran body not being able to withstand a few timely blows." She placed her hand against his shoulder. It warmed his skin. "You must have landed pretty hard on it."

He tried to look over his shoulder to see it but all he could see was her hand, small and slender, touching him. Her eyes spoke of concern when his met them.

"Do tell Jericho to go easier on you," she said with a small frown.

He slid off the table and grabbed his shirt. Everyone was always going easy on him. He was a soldier. He wanted to be treated like one, as though he was just one of the squad. He was tired of being singled out because he was royalty. Had Balt and Acer encountered similar problems during training? He couldn't imagine them paying attention to any order telling them to make the other soldiers go easier on them.

Putting his dark blue shirt on, Remi hid the pain it caused his shoulder and looked at Emmanuelle. She was still watching him, as though she expected an answer to what she'd said.

"No," he said it flatly, without any emotion, and held her gaze. "I have to go."

Emmanuelle watched him leave, knowing exactly where he was going to go. It was three months ago when she'd first noticed that he liked to think alone. She'd stumbled across him sitting staring out through the glass dome of the hydroponics deck of the ship. Whenever he was angry after coming to her, she always went there to watch him and ensure he was alright. She waited a few minutes and then walked through the ship, went up three levels, and walked out into the lush green of the deck. She loved it up here, with the flowers, grass and trees. They were all for research and to keep the air clean, but they were still beautiful. There wasn't this much green on all her home world.

He wasn't hard to find. She figured out which direction the Lyra system was in and found him sitting there, staring out of the window towards his home. She kept her distance so she didn't disturb him. She just wanted to check that he was alright and then she'd leave him alone. Why did he always stare towards home? Did he miss his planet and his family?

He touched his shoulder a few times, rolling it back occasionally. It was bothering him. If he'd stayed in sickbay a few moments more, she would have given him some medication for it and healed the skin. She hadn't wanted to push him though. The moment she'd met him, the first time he'd been placed on her inspection table, she'd realised that he was sensitive about his arm. He resented it somehow. She couldn't figure out why. Surely it was better than having no arm at all? He would have been discharged from the imperial army if that had happened. His family had paid dearly to have him patched up so he could continue with the squad.

A crackling noise came from the metallic grey communicator band around her wrist and she placed her hand over it to stifle the noise so he wouldn't hear. She frowned out of the window when she saw a ship approaching. It was a Lyran fighter. A glance at Remi revealed that he hadn't noticed it. He was too lost in his thoughts.

She wished she could do something to make him feel better about his arm and being here. She wasn't blind. He hated it when she called him by his title, but it really wasn't her place to call him by his real name, no matter how many times he insisted. It was unfair on him though. She called the others by their names—Jericho, Alessandro, Pietr, Ambra. The difference was, calling them by their names wouldn't get her discharged. To everyone on the ship, including his superiors, he was Lyra IV.

The doors to her right opened and a tall man entered, his build broad and muscular, and his dark blue flight suit stretched incredibly tight over his body like a second skin. He smiled, winked and nodded at her as he passed.

She blushed at the knowing edge to that smile. He wasn't flirting. He'd been telling her that he knew what she was up to—watching Remi.

She shrank back behind a tree and continued to watch him, as she always would.

The man approached him and the moment Remi turned to see who it was, he was on his feet. She was surprised when Remi hugged the man. There was an exchange of very manly back patting and then they broke apart. Now that they were standing together, she could see the similarities between them, although the newcomer was taller than Remi. They shared black hair and charming good looks, and bodies to die for.

The newcomer was one of his brothers. She looked at the window, replaying the sight of the fighter ship coming into dock. Was it Captain Lyra II or Captain Lyra III? She'd never met either of them, so she couldn't tell, and they all looked so similar—handsome, sinful and strong. She looked back at the men. Remi gave a sour gesture to his arm and then laughed when his brother said something. It was nice to see him smiling again.

She ducked behind the tree, breathing hard and desperate for Remi not to see her as they walked in her direction. They went past and Remi walked through the door. His brother said something and then turned back. Remi disappeared as the door closed.

Emmanuelle gasped when she realised the man was coming back to her. He caught her arm as she tried to dive out the other side of the bush and held her tightly, pulling her back towards him.

"Are you in the habit of spying on my brother?" His tone was low and dangerous. The smile that had been in his eyes a moment ago had disappeared. "What do you want with him?"

She shook her head when she realised that he thought she wanted to hurt Remi.

"It's not like that," she said quickly. "He came into my office hurt again today and I wanted to make sure he was alright."

"So you followed him?" The man's grip tightened and anger flashed in his pale blue eyes. Captain Lyra III. Out of the sons of Lyra, only he had eyes that colour.

"No, sir, I didn't follow him. He always comes here when he needs to think. I only wanted to make sure he was alright... he gets so depressed about his arm."

The man released her and his look shifted to reveal concern. "What's wrong with it?"

"Nothing." She suddenly felt as though she was saying more than she should on the subject. "It's fine, but he doesn't like it. He never has done."

"He's never said anything to me." There was an air of disbelief about him, and a hint of jealousy.

"He doesn't say anything to anyone. I only know because I'm the one who is close enough to see it in his eyes when he comes into my office."

"Your office?" He looked her over. "You're a nurse?"

She nodded.

"They never had nurses like you when I was going through training," he muttered darkly and frowned. "Do you take good care of my little brother?"

Emmanuelle nodded again. "I keep an eye on him. He's doing well in training but insists on getting hurt."

"Insists?" The man looked confused.

"Your brother can take care of himself, as can all the men here, but they seem to insist on getting hurt so they end up on my inspection table."

He gaze raked over her again, burning her. "I can't blame them."

She glared at him and pressed her hands against her hips.

"Do you pay such close attention to all your patients?" His head cocked to one side as though he was considering getting hurt too.

She hesitated and then nodded. Was it a capital crime to lie to royalty? She wasn't Lyran, but she did serve in their imperial army. Perhaps that gave her ties enough to Lyra to make it wrong.

"I do what I can to ensure all my patients get the help they need. Your brother is no exception."

He looked over his shoulder towards the door. "Then I ask you to make him the exception. I ask you to ensure my brother's happiness."

He walked away, leaving her confused and alone. Ensure his brother's happiness? She presumed he was talking about Remi's hatred of his cybernetic arm and not something else.

Remi frowned when his brother finally appeared. "What were you doing in there?"

Acer smiled. "Oh, you know, staring at the stars. It's a beautiful view. I hear you go there often."

His frown intensified. "Who told you that?"

"Does it matter?" Acer placed a hand on his shoulder. He winced. "She was right, you don't take good care of yourself."

"Who have you been speaking—" He cut himself off when it dawned on him. "Emmanuelle."

"If that's the name of your nurse, then yes, Emmanuelle." Acer's gaze shifted to his cybernetic arm. "She's only concerned about you. Many a man would be flattered to have such a beautiful woman's attention."

Remi turned his back and walked down the stairs to the lift. "I'm not special to her, if that's what you're insinuating. She's a good woman. She looks after us all. Just the other day Jericho—"

"Jericho is here?" Acer cut in. Remi could hear the disapproval in his voice. Acer blamed Jericho for what had happened to him during the Varkan insurgence, even though he'd repeatedly told Acer that it had been his own fault.

"Don't start," he said with a sigh and entered the lift. He pressed the button for the mess hall and watched the doors slide closed. "He's a good friend and a good man. I wish you'd quit blaming him already. I told you it was my fault for not being cautious enough. I've learned my lesson, alright? Let it go."

Acer frowned at him. He knew he sounded snappish and angry, but he was tired of going over the same subject every time they met up. His brother leaned past him and pressed another button. Remi looked up at him.

"I just need to check something on my ship. I came straight to see you," Acer said with an affectionate smile.

It had been a long time since they'd seen each other, although they communicated regularly. The last time had been Sebastian's marriage and back then he'd been a whole person. He flexed the fingers on his left hand again and stared at it. He didn't know why he couldn't accept it was a part of him now. He wondered if he ever would.

"What else did she say?" Remi didn't take his eyes off his hand. He still had nightmares about the night he'd lost it. Not even Emmanuelle's kind words and light accepting touch could make those stop.

"That you insist on getting hurt." Acer laughed and shook his head, his smile broad. "I told her that I couldn't blame you. She really is a pretty one."

Remi couldn't deny that. Emmanuelle was beautiful. He'd never seen an angel like her.

The doors opened onto the cargo deck and Remi stepped out first. He looked at the people carrying ship parts through the airlock. There was a muffled curse and Acer strode past him. He hurried to keep up with him.

"Engineer Stella, I told you to be careful with those weapons!" There was anger in Acer's voice but Remi noticed it didn't touch his eyes. The look in them was soft, turning gentle as Acer watched the female engineer nod and continue with her work. Remi looked at the woman and then back at his brother.

"Not a nurse, but a pretty one all the same." He watched Acer closely to gauge his reaction.

His brother gave him a shrug and a look that lied and said he hadn't noticed.

"Balt transferred her from his ship for breaking the gravity drive. I won't be a minute." Acer walked away, disappearing through the airlock.

Remi looked at the engineer again. His brother couldn't fool him. He'd have to congratulate his older brother, Balt, for spotting a perfect woman for Acer. She was exactly his type—strong, intelligent, stubborn and dark haired. She'd be a wonderful handful that would get Acer's back up and make him fall for her.

Acer reappeared and stood beside him a moment.

"Are you alright?" he said.

Remi nodded. "I was just thinking. You did disturb my thinking after all."

"She watches you, you know." Acer turned his back to the ship. Remi noticed that the engineer glanced across at Acer. How would Acer react if he mentioned that he wasn't the only one a woman was watching?

"She also calls me Lyra IV." He turned away and walked back towards the lift. "I can't get her to call me Remi."

"Protocol, dear brother." Acer clapped his hand against his good shoulder. "It's the bane of us all."

Was it? Perhaps he and his brothers weren't so different after all. He led the way to the mess hall and entered second, allowing Acer to go first just so he could see the panicked scramble of every soldier in the room as they shot to their feet to salute him.

He wanted to be a captain and in charge of his own ship. There was such a power gap between lieutenant and captain. No one saluted him.

"I know that look," Acer said. "I had the same one when Balt visited me once during my early years in the army. You'll get there soon enough. It's in your blood. We sons of Lyra have a reputation for a reason... perfection is bred into us."

Remi shook his head and frowned. He raised his left hand and sighed. "I'm not perfect anymore, brother."

Acer took hold of his hand and looked it over. "Seems perfect to me. Quit moping or I'll have to have a word with that nurse of yours."

He cursed his brother for saying that loud enough to draw the attention of everyone in the room. His cheeks blazed and he added a curse aimed at himself for reacting like a child would to such unwelcome attention. So what if he liked Emmanuelle. He was a man. He was flesh and blood and had needs and desires like any other man in the universe. If asked, he'd be the first to admit that he wanted her for his own. It wasn't as though he was hiding his attraction. Everyone in his squad knew he got hurt with the intention of getting himself into her office again.

He'd gone there today with nothing more than a case of bruising.

She never turned him away though.

He'd seen her turn others away for such petty wounds.

He chose a seat in the corner and Acer sat beside him. He listened to his brother relaying the tale of his last battle in space and it wasn't long before they had an audience. Acer was as charming towards the women and as brash towards the men as usual. It was good to see him again. He looked down at his left hand. Perhaps his brother and Emmanuelle were right. His arm hadn't changed who he was. In fact, he couldn't imagine life without it now. He'd grown strangely used to the superior strength in it and had learned to differentiate between his two hands so he didn't crush things with his left hand when using both.

Acer laughed about something and everyone laughed with him. Remi realised that he was talking about him. It was the first time Remi had tried to fly something coming up all over again. He went to stop him but Acer held up a hand.

"Come, brother, don't be shy. In a few weeks they'll send you to the pilot academy and everyone will discover the dirty secret of your first flight and crash landing into the palace ponds," Acer said with another laugh.

He leaned back in his chair, letting Acer have his way.

Just as Acer was about to tell them, the alarms sounded across the ship.

He looked up at the ceiling.

"All squadrons are to report for duty. This is not a drill. We have been issued orders and are en route to Varka Two."

His blood ran cold. Varka Two? His gaze fell to his arm. Was he strong enough to go back there? He'd learnt a lot in the past few years, but was it enough to keep him alive? The Varkans were fierce fighters and had some of the most advanced military equipment in the universe.

Everyone scrambled to their posts and the room was empty in a matter of seconds. He looked at Acer.

"Maybe we'll get to spend more time together soon." His brother stood and placed a hand on his shoulder. "I'd better return to my ship. We'll have to detach before you make the shift to full speed."

Remi stood and nodded, trying to be strong. Acer pulled him into a hug and Remi closed his eyes as he held him in return.

"Take care, little brother." Acer released him, turned away and walked out the door.

He was alone.

He looked at the empty room and fought the fear inside himself. He was stronger now and far more skilled. The Varkans wouldn't get the better of him.

When the ship shifted to full speed, he left the room and went to find his squadron. They would leave the ship before it reached Varka Two, each squadron entering the atmosphere in their own set of ships. There were three for each squadron. He'd be in the one with Alessandro, Jericho, Pietr and Ambra, as he always was.

He reached the cargo deck and crossed it towards the dock where his ship waited. The window of the airlock where his brother's ship had been docked showed nothing but empty space now. He would see his brother again. He had no doubt about that.

Everyone was gathered at the far end of the cargo bay, waiting for orders. He found Jericho and Ambra in one corner.

"How's it looking?" He nodded towards the captains. The six men were closely huddled together, talking about something. They were probably discussing tactics and information. One day he'd be a part of that group. One day.

"Like war, only worse," Jericho said and Ambra gave him a worried look. Jericho grinned and grabbed her around the waist, pulling her up to him.

"Nothing to worry about, I won't let the nasty Varkans anywhere near you, sweets."

She frowned and pushed him off her. Remi wished they'd both get it over with and admit they were in love. Their constant playful jesting and teasing made it blindly obvious to everyone but them apparently. He noticed Ambra glance at Jericho, her cheeks flushed. Jericho gave her a wide grin.

Remi clenched his fists. "I won't let them near any of you."

"Those are fighting words." Jericho playfully punched him on the arm. He winced when his shoulder grated. Jericho look worried now. "You sure you're up for this? Maybe you should get your nurse to check you over one last time... real close like... an all over inspection from her could send a soldier to his death a happy man."

Ambra hit Jericho in the chest and glared.

Remi ignored him and the rest of his squadron as they joined in. His thoughts drifted to the nurse in question. Jericho was right in a way. He had to see her.

Everyone fell silent when the captains returned to their squadrons. Remi listened half-heartedly to the orders they were being given, his mind still on Emmanuelle. He couldn't leave for Varka Two without letting her know his feelings and discovering her own.

"You have thirty minutes to prepare for launch," his captain said and he looked up at him.

Thirty minutes.

He had to see her.

He pushed through the crowd, not answering Jericho's shouted questions as he focused on getting to her. He only had thirty minutes before he had to board the ship that would take him away from her to Varka Two. His shoulder was the perfect excuse to see her again.

He made his way up through the decks to her office. Its location was fixed in his mind now. He could find it blindfolded. Reaching the door, he knocked and it slid open.

"Lieutenant Lyra IV, I thought you'd be en route to Varka Two by now." There was a hint of nerves in her voice when she mentioned the name of the planet. She knew his file and knew that Varka Two was where he'd lost his arm. Her concern touched him and gave him the courage to continue.

"I left in a hurry earlier and didn't let you finish your work on my shoulder. I thought it best to get it checked out completely before I go into battle."

He sat on her inspection table, nerves turning his stomach. She put down the computer pad she had been reading and walked over to him. Her thigh brushed his knee as she stopped close to him.

"You'll have to take your shirt off." There was a hint of seduction to her voice, a low sensuality that made him warm inside. Her fingers brushed his neck by his collar and worked downwards towards the buttons of his shirt. Clearly she wasn't expecting him to undress himself this time.

His heart accelerated when she leaned towards him, her hands grazing his arms as she pulled his shirt down them. Her shoulder pressed against his chest and he tilted his head towards her, closing his eyes as he breathed in her soft perfume.

"Call me Remi," he whispered into her ear. She tensed and paused at her work. When she straightened up slightly, her mouth was close to his. He could feel her breath against his face, unsteady and trembling. She stayed there a moment before moving away.

He watched her fiddling with the instruments on the tray. He was making her nervous. Did that mean she liked him too? He should've asked his brother how to read women. He'd never been any good at it.

Emmanuelle teetered on the brink of calling him Remi as he'd asked her to. It wasn't her place though. She couldn't break the rules. The army was her home now. If they discharged her she had nowhere to go. It wasn't only that. She didn't want to leave this place. She didn't want to leave Remi.

He preened his black hair back, long fingers pushing the wavy tendrils of it from his face. It was longer on top than she remembered, but still short at the back.

Picking up the scanner, she walked around him, consciously brushing his knee with her hip as she passed. He breathed in sharply and his eyes followed her, burning her body with their heat and hunger. She brought her hand up and stroked it over his shoulder as she came to stand behind him. He kept his head turned to the side but closed his eyes. How much time did they have? How long would it be before he was gone? Fear whispered to her heart. She didn't know if he'd come back this time. Had he learnt enough over these past two years to keep himself alive on that hellish planet?

Tears filled her eyes but she suppressed them, focusing on her work. She ran the scanner over his shoulder. The skin around the graze was bruising now, darkening and becoming mottled. The scan revealed no fractures or anything out of the ordinary. He'd probably jarred it or it was merely stiff from the bruising.

She didn't dare move into clear view of him while there were tears in her eyes. It would only worry him and make her look weak. She'd been through so much in her life. Now wasn't the time to cry. If he left here worrying about her, it would impact on his focus while he was down on the planet. She knew that he thought about her, that he had feelings for her. She'd realised it shortly after meeting him. The fact that he found reasons to see her at least three or four times a week had made it obvious.

Reaching around him, she picked up the skin healing device and ran the red beam over his flesh. The bruising disappeared. Now all she had to do was give him a dose of painkillers and he'd be on his way. Her twin hearts beat in opposition of that thought and the idea of him going into battle. She'd seen the fallout of war and the casualties it left in its wake. She didn't want that to happen to Remi.

"All done," she whispered and placed her hand against his back. He tensed and then relaxed again. His body was warm beneath her fingers and she traced them downwards, following the line of his right shoulder blade. He had a strong back and an amazing body that put all others she'd seen to shame. It was no wonder the sons of Lyra had a reputation. Now two of them were married, leaving only Remi and his older brother Acer to be caught. She'd seen the looks the female soldiers gave Remi. All of them wanted him. They wanted to catch him.

A jealous snake hissed in her ear that they couldn't have him. He was hers. It was her who he came to every time he was hurt. It was her who healed him and helped him through his dark times.

She moved around him, keeping close so her hip brushed his knees again. His hands flexed against the edge of the inspection table, fingers indenting the black leather.

"Not leaving?" She placed the healing device back onto the tray along with the scanner. She looked up when he didn't answer, straight into dark passionate eyes. Her mouth turned dry and the twin beat of her hearts threatened to make her dizzy. His gaze fell to her lips. Hers dropped to his body. Bad move. Every muscle of it was tensed as he gripped the table. It was a divine sight worthy of the gods' notice and it made her hum with desire inside.

"Emmanuelle," he whispered, husky and low and full of desire.

She tried to swallow. Her throat was too dry and sticky.

His left hand rose.

Her eyes closed and she kept her head lowered as his fingers caressed her cheek. It surprised her on two fronts. One, that he had finally discovered the courage to touch her and two, that he was using his cybernetic arm to do so. His hand opened, palm cupping her cheek. The feel of his thumb sweeping across her lower lip was too much. Desire jolted through her, sparking along every nerve. She lowered her head further, feeling the change in her and unable to stop her long silver hair from floating upwards in response to the strong emotions surging through her.

"What the..." His hand raised her head up. She squeezed her eyes shut and tried to get control of herself again. She couldn't. The feelings were too strong. Her hair danced in the air, her hearts revelling in his touch. "I've always meant to ask you where you're from. I guess I have to now."

She opened one eye and then the other and looked at him. The blush blazed across her cheeks when she saw the fascination in his eyes. Gathering her hair, she tried to smooth it down but it refused to stay put. She always responded strongly to her feelings and her hair always insisted on showing it. It was just something that happened to all her species.

"Dazkara." Her voice trembled with nerves, and she smiled with relief when she finally managed to make her hair behave. "It... I..."

He smiled and caught her cheek again. Her hair rebelled against her command to stay put.

"Don't be ashamed. It's amazing. You're amazing. I'd thought you were an angel of Iskara."

She laughed and then pretended to clear her throat when he looked offended and frowned.

"Angel? Dazkarans are bloodthirsty and destructive. Our home planet is an arid desert because our forefathers annihilated every living creature and plant. I'm no angel," she whispered the last part.

He caught her other cheek, his hands cool against her burning flesh. She couldn't tear her eyes away from his. There was such sincerity in them.

"You are an angel, Emmanuelle. No doubt about it. I've never met anyone as kind and beautiful as you."

Her hair rose a little higher in response to that, her twin hearts fluttering against her chest. She blinked rapidly. What did he expect her to say in response? There was nothing she could say. There was only one way to repay him for such sweet words.

She stepped towards him, intent on kissing him, and lost her nerve the moment her hips nudged his knees apart. He continued for her, luring her towards him with his hands and shifting forwards on the table at the same time. Her breath trembled along with the rest of her body when his lips neared hers.

An alarm sounded.

The soldiers had fifteen minutes before they had to report in.

She drew back and stared at Remi, suddenly aware of what they'd been about to do and unsure whether she could go through with it. She'd put his mind at ease. He wouldn't worry about her while he was fighting now and he was healed. There was nothing left for her to do. Perhaps when he came back, she would let him see her true feelings. She wasn't brave enough right now.

"You should go." She went to turn away.

"You're not getting away that easily." He grabbed her wrist, dragging her back to him. Her thigh knocked against the table between his legs. Before she could form a protest, his mouth descended on hers, claiming her lips in a fiery kiss that stole her ability to speak.

She leaned into the kiss, her hands coming up to press against his bare chest as she closed her eyes. It was incredible. She tiptoed, wanting to get closer to him. His arms went around her waist and settled on her backside, lifting her a little off the floor. Her hair swirled around them, tickling her face. She definitely couldn't control it now. The desire rising inside her and the intense need that chased it placed everything beyond her control. She surrendered to Remi's demanding kiss and melted into his embrace, letting him take over.

Fifteen minutes and then he'd leave her. Fifteen minutes and he'd be going into battle on a planet that had almost claimed his life. These fifteen minutes had to count. She had to know his feelings for her and show him her own. This could be the last time she saw him.

She pushed away her morbid thoughts and focused on the rough glide of his lips over hers. Their tongues met and she fought for dominance over his, playing with it and driving him on.

Remi pushed her back and breathed hard. She was incredible. She matched him strength for strength, passion for passion. He ran his fingers through her hair, still amazed at the fact it reacted to her feelings. There was so much about her that he didn't know, but he wanted to find out. He longed for more time with her and swore that he would do his best on Varka Two so he could return to her.

In one swift move, his feet hit the floor and he lifted her onto the inspection table. Her eyes went wide with shock, as though she was surprised to find herself suddenly on the padded leather bench. He grabbed her backside and dragged her towards the edge of the table, settling himself between her legs. Her hands rested on his shoulders, fingers gently grazing his skin, sending his temperature soaring.

He pulled her against him again and kissed her, hard and with all the passion burning inside him. Only fifteen minutes. It wasn't enough time. He wanted to make love to her, to spend the rest of his life showing her just how special she was and how beautiful.

His hand slid up to her waist and hers dropped to his upper arms, thumbs caressing the curve of his biceps. For a moment, he'd thought she was going to stop him. Taking her compliance and touch as an invitation, he raised his hands a little more, until they moulded around the firm globes of her breasts. She moaned into his mouth, her kiss turning fierce and hungry. It was a battle to remain in control, to fight her for dominance. It seemed the fifteen minute deadline had filled her with the same urgency that he felt.

He squeezed her breasts, groaning internally at the feel of them and the fact he was finally touching her, and then moved to the buttons of her dress. Breaking the kiss, he drew back and watched his hands as he started to unbutton the dark blue dress. She leaned back, reached to the side towards the control panel and pressed a button. The door lock clicked into place. When he looked at her, she gave him a shy smile and blushed. That was a definite invite.

His fingers shook when he peeled apart the top half of her dress to reveal the inner curves of her pale breasts. He continued to undo the buttons, his heart beating faster with each one that gave and his erection growing harder. It pressed against his trousers, begging to be released. He wriggled to get it into a more comfortable position and the action spread Emmanuelle's legs further apart. The last button on her dress came undone. His gaze raked over her slim body, from her ripe small breasts to her toned stomach and finally her dark blue panties.

A groan left him, followed by a low guttural noise as he dragged her towards him and kissed her hard. He wanted her, wanted to stake his claim and make her wholly his at last. Her tongue fought his again and this time he won, leaning her over backwards and sliding his hands into her dress. The feel of her skin was amazing—soft and warm and supple. It gave under his fingers as he pressed them in, holding her tight.

His lips left hers and he kissed a trail down to her neck, tasting her warm flesh and scent of Lyran lilies. He continued downwards to her chest and brushed the two sides of her dress apart to reveal her breasts in their entirety. The pale mounds were peaked with small dusky nipples that called to him. He lowered his mouth to one and licked it before sucking it into his mouth.

She moaned and leaned back further, her hands on his shoulders stopping her from falling onto the table.

"Remi," she whispered and he stopped and drew back to look at her. The sound of his name spoken in such an aroused tone made his cock ache. He needed to be inside her.

A five minute warning sounded.

"No time..." She pulled herself up.

He jumped when her hands went to his belt and suddenly his trousers were falling down around his ankles. Clearly, she'd read his mind. All reasonable thought was chased from his head when she freed his hard length and ran her hand down it.

Emmanuelle told herself that she was crazy to be rushing into this but nothing in her life had ever felt as right. She stroked his long shaft again, desperate for it to be inside her. They only had five minutes. She couldn't let him leave this room without consummating what was fast becoming a relationship. It was a sending off present to him. It seemed like a reasonable excuse for the fact she was about to let him screw her on her inspection table.

Her panties were gone before she could blink.

The fire in his eyes said that he wasn't planning on leaving without having her either.

His hands claimed her backside, drawing her to the edge of the padded table and closer to him. He stepped up to her, nestling his hips between her legs. Her hands went to his shoulders, her eyes meeting his. He moved closer and the head of his cock brushed her slick opening. Her lips parted in a sigh that she felt in her whole body as he eased into her.

"Slow is going to have to come later," he said and she saw the apology in his eyes.

She nodded, knowing that he'd keep that promise when he came back and this battle was over. He always came back to her. This time wouldn't be any different.

She closed her eyes and moaned when he pulled out and thrust into her, hard and deep. Her fingertips dug into his shoulders, holding onto him as he pounded her roughly, the head of his length striking deep inside her. She tensed around him, moaning at the feel of him inside her, thrusting over and over with such intensity that she was sure they were both going to come undone before long.

Her hands dropped to his elbows and then slid down his forearms when she fell backwards onto the inspection table. His hands claimed her waist, gripping her hips as he drove into her, moaning with each thrust. She arched her back and moaned with him, her knees rising to clamp his hips before her legs wrapped around him.

"Cruskin..." he muttered and she moaned a concurrence. This was too good.

Her eyes opened and she looked at him, holding his gaze and drowning in the feelings she could read in it. He thrust harder, making her breasts wobble and the bench squeak beneath her. She reached over her shoulders and grabbed the bench, holding on for dear life as he pounded her. Close. Closer.

Fire and lightning rushed through her, a bright light exploding in front of her eyes. She arched off the table and clamped her muscles down on his hard length as the blaze reached there. He screamed out his orgasm, thrusting deep inside her. Her thighs trembled against his. His hands shook against her waist. She realised he was breathing as fast as she was, so hard that her head spun.

She looked at him. His eyes were wide, his mouth hanging open, and his face was pale. He looked stunned.

"Gyaa—" he uttered and then collapsed to his knees.

"Remi!" she said and was immediately on the floor beside him.

Remi leaned forwards, trembling and panting. His hands pressed into the floor to support his weak body.

He'd never felt anything like that. Never. The moment she'd climaxed, her whole body had shimmered and a rush of warm electricity had bolted through him, driving him into his own orgasm. It had sent his mind reeling, spinning so fast that he felt as though he'd taken some intense drug. He stared at the floor, a little dazed and strangely relaxed.

"Remi?" She shook him by the shoulder.

He slowly turned his head to face her, his vision a little wobbly. Several of her danced in front of his eyes.

"Is it always like that?" He managed to get the words out.

She frowned, confused.

He drew another few breaths, gathering his strength and his senses.

"When you... this insane energy went through me... I... heh... in Iskara's name that was good." He grinned at her, pressed one hand into her shoulder and grabbed the inspection table with the other, hauling himself onto his feet.

His eyebrows rose when she pulled his underwear and trousers up for him. His legs were jelly and he was forced to lean against the table for support, unable to trust himself to stand unaided. She straightened up, still gloriously naked between the two sides of her dress. Her cheeks were dark red, the colour of Koji.

"Does that always happen?" he said again, his heart slowing to an almost normal speed. It was a struggle, but after several attempts he managed to fasten his trousers and did his belt up.

She hesitated a moment and then looked up at him. Embarrassment filled her eyes. He caught her cheek with his left hand, unafraid of his arm now. It was a part of him and it hadn't stopped the most beautiful girl in the galaxy from wanting him. A beautiful and very special girl. What other tricks did she have up her sleeve? Right now, he felt as though he'd drunk a bottle of Koji and had chased it with a bottle of Aquan.

"I don't know," she whispered and then found her voice. "I've only ever been with Dazkarans... it seemed perfectly normal."

He smiled, trying to chase away her awkwardness.

"Why are you embarrassed?" His hand held her when she tried to look away, keeping her eyes locked with his. "There's no reason to be ashamed. It was amazing... my mind's still reeling. I don't think I'm going to come down again until we reach Varka Two."

The smile that had been slowly appearing on her face disappeared at the mention of the planet he was heading for.

"I promise I'll come back." He drew her into his arms. Her warm body pressed against his and he could feel her heart beating. He frowned at the strange rhythm. Hearts. He could feel her hearts beating. He pressed a kiss to her silvery hair, tame now that her emotions had changed from positive to negative. "I'll fight for you."

Hot tears wet his chest in response to that and he held her tighter, his hand caressing her in the hope that it would calm her. She'd been close to tears earlier and had hidden it well. He didn't have the heart to say he'd noticed, or make her awkward again by making a fuss about her crying now. He just held her close and pressed kisses to her hair, savouring the feel of her in his arms.

The alarm sounded. All personnel were to report to the docks.

"I have to go," he whispered, his voice cracking and emotions making it impossible to speak any louder.

She took a deep breath and shuffled in his arms. He presumed she was wiping her tears away because when she emerged from his embrace, there wasn't a trace of them on her cheeks. Her grey eyes were red with them though. He brushed his fingers across her cheek and sighed.

Her eyes closed.

He leaned in and kissed her slowly, a promise of things to come when he returned. He would win her hearts completely. He would fight for her.

Her lips left his and he looked at her.

"I'll be waiting." Tears filled her eyes.

He pressed one last, long kiss to her lips and then turned away, grabbing his shirt as he passed it. He slipped it on before he reached the door. When he turned back, she'd already buttoned most of her dress. She pressed the button on the control panel to unlock the door for him and then gave him a shaky smile.

He smiled back at her, his heart aching. Raising his hand in a silent goodbye, he sighed and then walked away.

He would fight for her.

He would come back to her.

Emmanuelle looked out of the window, fear clenching her heart each time she saw a blast on the planet below. It was never ending. The battle had been raging for over three weeks now and she hadn't heard a word from the surface about how things were progressing. Casualties had been sent up and each time they were, her hearts thundered and screamed with fear. So far, none of Remi's squadron had been brought in. The nurse in the morgue on the surface had promised to contact her if he was brought in. The thought that she might receive the call at any time to say that he was dead made her hearts break. She took a deep breath and steeled herself, forcing herself to watch the fight happening far below her and sending prayers to the gods to protect him.

Another set of bright white explosions erupted across the dark surface of the planet, forming an arch of circles that quickly evaporated into nothing. She pressed her hands against the window, breathing hard and hoping that Remi was alright. She couldn't bear the thought of him fighting down there, battling for his life. It stole her sleep and her hunger. It had been days since she'd eaten anything substantial. Her superiors had expressed their concern and tried to cheer her up, but it just wasn't possible. There was only one person who could cheer her up now. Remi.

A fighter leaving the surface caught her eye. It was followed by one of the larger transport ships that the soldiers had gone to the surface in.

She stared at it, fearing that this time Remi would be in it.

The sound of the infirmary behind her came back, the noise of nurses and doctors rushing around and trying to save the lives of the soldiers clamouring in her ears. Duty called. She raced to help, assisting those that needed it most first. Most of the last group of patients to come from the surface were stable now. She helped the nurses move them out of the operating theatres and into the wards. They were quickly filling up. Someone would need to check all the patients and see which ones could be discharged to make more room.

The ship rocked as the fighter and transport vessel docked with it. Soon, the halls would be pandemonium as the new casualties were brought in. She finished hooking a man up to the bio-scanner and monitors above his bed and then went to her office. A quick clear up and she was ready for the next set of patients. She could handle any wounds that didn't require surgery. She swiped the beam of the sterilizing device over her tools, preparing them. Anything that was life-threatening had to be handled by the doctors. She had faith in them. They were some of the best in the fleet.

A murmur swept down the corridor, growing louder. The rush of feet followed it. Her hearts thundered as she waited to see if this time it would be Remi lying on her inspection table. She went out into the hall, watching the passing hover-stretchers as they were pushed by almost at a run. The clamour of voices reached a crescendo. The smell of blood filled the air. These soldiers were injured worse than any she'd seen so far. Most needed the doctors' attention. It was ghastly. Blood covered them and the wounds were deep. Some were missing limbs or were badly burnt. Her stomach churned. Fear pounded down on her.

She looked down the hall.

Her hearts almost stopped beating.

Remi.

Alessandro was supporting Remi as he hobbled down the hall, covered in blood.

She ran to him, her mind filling with his brother's words about protecting him. She had to help him. He needed her now more than ever. She grabbed his empty arm and gently placed it around her shoulders, helping Alessandro support him and leading the way to her office. Remi slumped against her. She gritted her teeth and forced him upwards, intent on supporting his weight and getting him to her table.

It seemed to take forever to get him into the room and there was no sense of relief when he was finally on the inspection table. He collapsed. She shouted for a nurse to assist Alessandro and then ran around the table to her tools. Leaning over Remi, she patted his cheek, faster and faster, matching her racing hearts. He murmured something, barely conscious.

"Remi, Remi... Remi!" she said, frantic and terrified by the sight of so much blood on him. It plastered his face and his clothes. There wasn't an inch of him that didn't seem to be coated in it. "Don't die on me!"

His hand weakly caught hers and stopped her from patting his cheek.

"I'll live for you instead," he croaked and frowned as he opened his eyes and looked at her. "I'm fine... Jericho."

She wasn't at all convinced that he was fine.

"What about him?"

"It's his blood... a Heavy Armour... it tore him apart. He didn't stand a chance." He threw an arm over his eyes and swallowed hard. His tight voice, laden with emotion, said that he was close to tears. It was understandable. He loved Jericho like a brother.

A noise in the hall made her look up, the sound of rushing feet and shouted commands.

"What about Ambra—" Her question seemed redundant when the doctors rushed past with a hover-stretcher, Ambra running behind them. Emmanuelle swallowed. The entire blanket covering the patient on the stretcher had been red with blood. There'd been life support equipment onboard.

"Jericho... he tried to protect Ambra. He... don't let him die. Do whatever you can for him... even if it's..." he trailed off and flexed his cybernetic hand. "I couldn't protect... we were separated... I was too late. I should've been there. It was my fault."

Emmanuelle held him down when he tried to sit up. He winced and pushed against her. She pushed back, determined not to let him aggravate his injuries and put his own life at risk.

"Calm down. It's not your fault, Remi," she whispered, her hand against his cheek. His tears dampened her fingertips and cut through the blood on his face.

"Whatever it takes..." He looked up at her, tears shining in his eyes. "Save him."

Tears filled her own eyes when she saw all the hurt in his. He and Jericho had been inseparable since the academy. They were closer than brothers.

"A normal soldier won't be given such treatment." It broke her heart to tell him that and see the realisation dawn in his eyes. Jericho would likely die.

He went to sit up again. She pushed him back down. Anger flashed in his dark eyes, red with tears.

"I'm a normal soldier like him! Like all of them!" He tried to push her away but she held him down. Her hands shook against him, trembling with fear as his whole face darkened. "Let me go!"

"No!" She pressed her hands against his shoulders and shoved him back down, pinning him against the table. "You're not a normal soldier. You're a prince, a son of Lyra. Your kingdom would do anything for you."

Fear shook her when his cybernetic hand closed tight around her wrist, making her bones creak. He gritted his teeth and pushed her away. She stumbled backwards and put a hand out behind her to grab the cupboards there and stop her from hitting them.

He was off the inspection table before she could stop him.

"They'll do this for me then!" He limped from the room and she followed him as he shoved people in the corridor aside and pushed through.

The gaps he'd made for himself closed behind him, hindering her. Before she could reach him, he was opening the doors to the operating theatre. She grabbed his arm and he turned on her. In his eyes, anger overruled pain.

"Leave me alone!" He pushed her hand off him. "Let me do this."

She grabbed him again, unwilling to give up that easily. She had to get him back to her inspection table before he passed out. It had to be purely adrenaline keeping him going now. "What are you going to do?"

He turned away and looked into the operating theatre. She looked past him at the doctors and Jericho where he lay on the table. A glance at Remi made her heart ache. The tears trembled on the brink of falling, his face ashen beneath the blood. The theatre lights reflected in his eyes. She could almost see Jericho in them. She didn't want to look at him. There was no way the doctors would be able to save him.

Remi swallowed and then frowned.

"Whatever it takes, understand?" he said when the doctors looked his way, voice showing none of the raw emotions she could see in his eyes. There was only determination and anger in it. "On my authority, do whatever it takes. If Jericho dies, I will never forgive you."

Ambra pushed past her and Emmanuelle was glad when Remi stopped her. He held Ambra close, his broad frame protecting her from the sight of Jericho. Ambra shook, trembling in Remi's arms.

"I won't let anything happen to him, Ambra." Remi held her closer. Emmanuelle stepped back to give them more room. "I'll bring him back for you, but he might not be the same."

Ambra looked up at him with wide eyes and understanding gradually dawned in them. She touched his cybernetic arm and forced a smile.

"I'll always love Jericho... always. It doesn't matter what it takes to save him. I'll always be there for him when he needs me."

Remi's hand covered hers and held it.

"Thank you Remi... I know that if it weren't for you... he'd be dead already," Ambra said with another smile, this one holding more feeling.

"I'll be there for you both—" He wavered on the spot, swallowed hard, and then collapsed to his knees.

Ambra looked horrified.

Emmanuelle rushed to his side, crouching close to him and placing her hand against his back. He wearily raised his head and looked at her. His pupils dilated and contracted, clearly struggling to focus.

"Will you let me attend to you now?" she whispered.

He nodded.

She pulled his arm around her shoulder and helped him stand with the aid of a male nurse.

"You were fooling nobody by saying you were fine," she muttered and took him back to her office.

It was an effort to get him onto the inspection table and lay him down. The weight of him drained her strength and she was breathing hard when she finally ducked out from under his arm. She carefully opened his armoured jacket and his shirt. He grimaced when she made him sit up again so she could remove them completely. They dropped to the floor at her feet.

Several men in black rushed past her office. One stopped in the doorway. The intricate white logo emblazoned on the left side of his chest told her that he was a bio-engineer.

She grabbed the scanner and ran it over Remi's torso.

"Does Lieutenant Lyra IV need anything?" the man said.

She shook her head. "I can handle him and his arm is fine."

The man nodded and left. She pressed the button on the control panel and closed the door so she wouldn't be disturbed again. Running the scanner over Remi's legs revealed that he had a weapons fire wound on his left thigh and his right knee was badly damaged. There was a burn mark and hole in his right upper arm too, and several lacerations across his stomach. It was nothing she couldn't repair or aid towards recovery. His knee would be the hardest. All she could do for it was use the binder to bring the flesh together again and then bandage it. It was down to his body to heal that one.

He winced and muttered something. She pressed a hand to his forehead. His skin was red hot and damp with sweat. He was becoming feverish. Picking up the injection gun, she loaded it with painkillers and then pressed it against the side of his arm. She fired it and he winced again before sleepily opening his eyes to look at her. Her fingers brushed his cheek and she smiled at him.

"Rest," she said and his eyes closed and then opened again, as though he was fighting the effect of the drug. "I won't let anything happen to you, Remi."

His eyes closed. She checked his vitals on the large monitor above the head end of the inspection table to her left and then set to work. It was going to be a long night. She only hoped that the bio-engineering team would be able to save Jericho.

She picked up the skin healing device and ran it over the cuts on his stomach and any other shallow wounds she could see. When they were closed, she carefully removed his trousers and boots, leaving him in only his underwear. She blushed when she remembered when they'd last been in this room together and then forced those thoughts out of her head. It wouldn't do to get distracted now. She had to focus so she could save him. One mistake could cost him his knee. If they had to replace it, it would be months before he would be allowed to return to duty. He'd miss his chance to enter the pilot academy. She knew how important that was to him, and how important it was that he entered there as just another soldier. No doubt his parents could get him in at any point in the course if he missed the start, but it wouldn't be what Remi wanted. He wanted to be treated as a normal soldier. Normal soldiers couldn't jump in mid-way through a course.

Healing the smaller cuts on his legs, she paused briefly at his knee to check on it. The wound was deep enough to reveal bone. It needed to be healed quickly to avoid more blood loss or permanent damage. She placed the skin healer down and picked up the next device. The instant she ran the blue beam over his knee, the bone began to disappear, his flesh knitting back together. It wasn't a perfect solution, but the blood vessels and muscles would heal given a few weeks rest.

She stifled a yawn as the hours drew on and she stood holding the device. It was slow work and she was beginning to tire. There were still another two wounds to fix. She glanced at them, checking they weren't bleeding, and then looked up at his face. It was ashen. The image of his body on the monitor said he was stable, but the sight of him so pale and drawn made her worry. The device in her hands beeped and she looked down to see that it had finished its job. She applied some salve to his knee and then bandaged it.

Another hour and she'd healed the wound on his other leg and his upper arm. She placed the device down, dragged a stool over, and slumped onto it, ready to collapse.

Her fingers smoothed the hair from his forehead, stroking it gently. The medication would keep him asleep for a few hours more yet and then she'd give him another dose. The hall outside her office had gone quiet. She leaned over and pressed a kiss to Remi's lips, and then folded her arms on the table beside him and rested her head on them. She wanted to keep an eye on him but it was impossible to keep them open. Closing her eyes, she yawned and drifted away.

Remi frowned and then internally grimaced when he tried to move and found he couldn't. He focused, feeling groggy and weak, and tried to figure out what was happening. Slowly, feeling in his hands and feet returned. Pain burned in his knee and his right arm. He swallowed it and blinked his eyes open. The lights were too bright. He squinted and then smiled inside when the fuzzy shape of Emmanuelle gradually came into focus.

She leaned over him, running the healing device over something. His knee. Now that his head was clearing, he could feel the warm tickle of the red beam over his skin.

It gradually turned from a warm tickle to a burning pain.

He grimaced and flexed his fingers into fists.

"Keep still," she whispered, voice soothing and gentle as always. It warmed his heart to hear the concern and affection in it.

She put the device down on the table near his feet and walked up to him. His eyes followed her every move and he frowned when she picked up an injection gun and loaded it with a clear liquid.

"Don't knock me out again," he croaked, throat parched and sore.

She smiled and her grey eyes shone with it. Her fingers brushed his forehead and he closed his eyes at the calming touch.

"It's only a painkiller."

Remi flinched when she shot the injection into his neck.

The whole world suddenly seemed more hazy and warm. He looked up at her, smiling dazedly as the heat rushed through him to fill every inch of his body. His head felt fuzzy. He felt like he had after their moment together.

"Better?" Emmanuelle whispered close to his face, her soft breath fanning his skin.

He nodded and then frowned when she disappeared, walking back down to his knee. She picked up the device and ran the red beam over his leg again. This time he didn't feel a thing.

He watched her for a while, too dazed by the drug to think straight. When his head cleared, leaving only his body numb to pain, he remembered why he was here and what had happened.

"Jericho?" Remi couldn't say anything more for fear of his emotions getting the better of him.

She looked at him with such worry that he could feel her anxiety reflected inside him.

His heart clenched, fear crushing it as a whispered voice in his head said that Jericho was dead. He went to sit up, but she was too fast for him and her hands were pressing him back down onto the padded table before he could move an inch.

"He's stable," she said and relief bolted through him. It only lasted a moment before his better sense said that stable didn't mean safe. "They're having to do more work."

"How much?"

She returned to his knee and continued with her work.

She was quiet for a few minutes and then looked at him. "Over fifty percent of his original body has been lost. They've had to integrate him fully into a cybernetic body. It's not advanced. The muscles... the body... it's passable... but..."

He got the impression from her pale face and wandering eyes that she didn't want to say anything more. How bad was it? It had been hard enough for him to come to terms with his arm. How would Jericho cope with losing his entire body? What had he done to Jericho? He should've let him die. He'd been so blind to his friend's feelings. What if Jericho hated him for what he'd done?

"But?" He needed to hear the extent of the damage.

"His head is a different matter. It could be years before we have technology advanced enough to recapture how he'd looked. They've resorted to modifying one of the androids heads."

He felt sick. The androids were barely advanced. Their bodies were bulky like Heavy Armour and their heads were almost robotic in appearance. They resembled the helmets he'd worn into battle to shield his face.

"Iskara..." he whispered, unable to say anything more.

Emmanuelle's fingers played softly against his cheek and he looked up at her, not hiding any of his feelings. She sighed and leaned over him, her body covering his as she held him. It comforted him more than anything could have at that moment. He raised heavy fuzzy arms to hold her and closed his eyes. She was warm against him, soft and soothing.

"He won't hate you," she whispered against his bare chest. "Jericho is strong. He'll be grateful that you did all you could to save him. It's not him I'm worried about."

She drew back and looked into his eyes.

"It's Ambra. I don't know how she'll take it."

Would Jericho forgive him as easily as Emmanuelle thought he would? His friend had always envied his arm, saying how much he wanted cybernetic parts so he could be the best soldier there was. Would he say that still when he awoke to find he was more than half cybernetic?

The look in Emmanuelle's eyes demanded he say something to allay her fears. She was worried about Ambra almost as much as she worried about him.

With a lot of effort, he managed to cup her cheek and smiled. The drug made it hard to move and almost impossible to control the strength in his arm.

"Ambra will be fine. She'll always love Jericho, regardless of what he looks like," he said and she straightened. He caught her wrist to stop her from going back to her work. "Has she seen him?"

She shook her head.

"I want to be with her when she does."

She nodded. "I'll tell them. She wanted to see you."

She handed him a clear blue bottle and he realised it was water. He pushed himself up a little and gulped it down as she helped him hold it. The cold was soothing and refreshing.

"Is she still outside?" he said when he was done and Emmanuelle took the empty container.

She laughed and shook her head. "You've been asleep for over three days. I think she's with some of the other female soldiers today, on the hydroponics deck. The doctors suggested they talked."

"Therapy, huh?" Remi sighed, recalling how much he'd hated the months of therapy, both physical and psychological, that he'd been put through after losing his arm.

She nodded again. "It's good for them to talk. Ambra needs female companionship right now. I can't imagine... actually I can... I can imagine how hard it has been for her."

A tear streaked down her cheek. He reached out to her, wanting her to come to him and hating the fact that he couldn't go to her. She kept her distance, staring at the floor.

"I was so scared, Remi." Emmanuelle looked across at him. It broke his heart to see the tears in her eyes. "I thought I was going to lose you... I couldn't stop thinking about you, fearing that the next call I received would tell me you'd died."

He reached out again, less patient this time, flexing his fingers as best he could to make her come to him.

"I said I'd fight for you and I'd come back to you. I wasn't planning on being dead when that happened."

His words only made her cry harder. He cursed himself and pressed against the padded table, forcing himself up into a sitting position. His knee protested and ached, sending pain shooting up his leg.

"Idiot!" she snapped and tried to push him back down.

Ignoring her feeble attempts to stop him from getting up, he lowered his legs over the edge of the table and grabbed her, pulling her into his arms.

"Shh," he whispered into her hair as she sobbed against his chest, curled up with her hands pressed to it. He stroked her hair and held her close, making a silent promise to never let her go. "I said I'd come back... although I'm a little broken."

A giggle rose from the depths of his embrace.

"I was fixing you," she mumbled against his skin, warming it with her breath. She tried to wrestle free of his arms but he held her, unwilling to relinquish her now that he had her. It had taken a phenomenal amount of effort and had given him a lot of pain to sit up. He wasn't about to waste it all by letting her go so quickly.

He kissed her hair and then her forehead, gradually working his way down to her mouth. She looked up at him and then closed her eyes when he leaned in to kiss her. Their lips barely touched, sending a warm shiver through him and filling his heart with tranquillity and happiness. On the planet, he'd feared that her feelings would have changed when he came back to her. The thought of that had scared him more than the Varkans.

"If I were in Jericho's shoes." He opened his eyes and met hers. "Would you still... I mean... if you do, I don't know if you do, but if you do... would you still love me?"

Her pink cheeks darkened and she dropped her gaze to his chest for a moment before meeting his eyes again.

"I would... it's the man you are that I fell in love with, not your appearance... although..." Her blush deepened. "There's nothing wrong with your looks."

He smiled at her, glad that she would love him regardless and thrilled that she'd admitted her feelings for him. She tried to make him lie down again. He refused, catching her hands in his and holding them.

"How long am I going to be stuck with you?" he said to her hands.

"About two weeks and then you'll be fine. You'll be healed before you start at the academy."

He brushed his thumbs across her knuckles. Her hands were so small and delicate but they worked such wonders.

"And how long do you want to be stuck with me?" He smiled and raised his eyes to meet hers. "Does forever sound alright?"

Her cheeks blazed again but this time she didn't avert her eyes. She held his gaze, sure and steady.

"Forever?" Emmanuelle said with a mock frown, stringing him along and teasing him. She pulled a thoughtful face. He frowned for real. The smile rose to her lips, breaking free of its restraints. "Forever sounds good... but..."

"But?" His frown didn't shift. His dark eyes grew a little blacker.

"You're a prince of Lyra. I don't think your family would like you going out with a nurse."

He shrugged and parted his legs. She rolled her eyes when he pulled her up against him, accidentally knocking his knee in the process and causing a grimace to compress his lips. He could pretend all he liked that he was fine but she knew that sitting as he was caused his knee pain.

"I don't care what they think." There was a beautiful honesty in his eyes. "No one stopped Balt from marrying his slave girl, or Sebastian from marrying the woman he ran away with, and no one will stop me—"

Her eyes widened. He wasn't insinuating what she thought he was. A deep look into his eyes revealed that he was.

"We barely know each other." She placed her hands against his chest. It seemed like a valid excuse to take things a little slower. Unfortunately, from what she'd heard, none of his brothers had taken things slow. Balt and Sebastian had married their wives barely a week after meeting them. Slow just wasn't their style.

"Oh, I think we know each other pretty well," he whispered, eyes full of meaning that his sultry smile backed up.

She blushed again and cursed him for making her react that way all the time. So they'd had sex and she'd admitted that she had feelings for him, loved him no less, but that didn't mean they had to get married right this minute.

"I... need time," she blurted out and he frowned. "Your training starts in barely a few weeks time. You need to focus on healing and your studies."

His frown tightened.

"I thought you—" he started and she cut him off by clamping her hand down over his mouth.

"I do... I really do... but I wasn't expecting this."

Hurt surfaced in his eyes.

Her hearts ached. She had to say something to make him feel better and make him see that she did want to marry him, just not this second. They were still in the middle of a war and he couldn't throw his dream of becoming a pilot away like she knew he would if he married her. She wanted him to become one and follow in his brothers' footsteps as he wanted to.

"I'll marry you," she said and his eyes brightened. She felt him smile against her palm. "I'll marry you when you can fly me, yourself, to Dazkara to tell my family."

He pushed her hand away, dragged her up against his chest, and kissed her breathless.

She took that as a yes.

Remi paced nervously along the dock in front of the small fighter. He locked his hands behind his back and stared at the floor, slowly losing his patience as the anticipation and excitement ate away at him. She'd promised. She'd said that she'd be here. Where was she?

He looked up when someone entered and turned to pace back along the dock when he saw it was two of his older brothers, Balt and Acer. Not Emmanuelle. Where was she? Wasn't she coming? She'd been at the graduation ceremony. He was a pilot now and he had a promise to keep. So did she. It had only taken him six months to qualify as a pilot, faster than anyone in his class. He'd graduated with the previous class.

"Relax." Acer smirked and slapped his shoulder. "You look a little desperate."

Remi shot him a glare. His nerves threatened to overwhelm him. He took deep breaths and let them go slowly, trying to calm himself. She'd come, just as she'd promised. He'd take her to Dazkara and then they'd return to Lyra Prime to be married. He'd already arranged everything. She couldn't back out now. He hadn't let her out of his sight for the past few months for this reason. He had to marry her. She had to be his.

He'd had her transferred to the academy medical team just so he could stay near her and they could share accommodation. He'd spent each night with her in his arms, had awoken this morning to see her face. Now he needed to see her more than ever.

The door at the end of the dock opened again. He looked up, shoulders tensed, and then relaxed again when he saw it was Jericho and Ambra. He was glad to see them together again. Jericho had been a nightmare since the battle on Varka Two and his integration into the cybernetic body. He'd turned his back on Ambra, convinced that she couldn't love him and that she deserved better, and had ignored everyone when they'd told him that Ambra still loved him. He'd even ignored Ambra. At least now they'd worked things out.

Remi was breaking with tradition at the wedding and borrowing something from Kayla's species' history. It was called a 'best man'. From how Kayla had explained it, he'd got the impression that it was someone to support you on the day and someone you were close to. He wanted Jericho to be that man.

"I thought we were seeing the happy couple off," Jericho said, the smile evident in his voice even if the dark visor of his new face didn't shift to show it. "Ambra was panicking that we'd be late. She stood you up?"

Remi turned his glare on him. "No... I'm sure she's just late."

"You sure?" Ambra said, hanging off Jericho's arm and grinning. "Maybe she got cold feet –"

"Why would she do that?" he barked.

"I've seen your flying... it gives me the chills." She laughed and hid behind the bulky mass of Jericho when Remi tried to grab her.

Remi sighed and then went still when the door opened again, this time behind him. The steady tap of boots on the metal walkway rang in his ears, a step so light that it could only be her.

"She's beautiful." Her soft voice caressed his ears and warmed his heart.

He turned and looked at Emmanuelle.

"She certainly is," he whispered, turning her comment about the fighter towards her, and caught her wrist, pulling her close to him. "I thought you were standing me up."

She giggled and stepped out of his embrace. When she twirled on the spot, his attention fell to her clothes.

"I had to change." She ran her hands down her sides and over her hips, following the line of the snug blue flight suit. "Acer gave me it. He said that you didn't fly in a fighter without one."

Her grey gaze fell to his body and a half smile tugged at the corner of her lips. There was a hint of sensuality about the soft curve of it and the way her eyes raked over him.

"They're a little revealing." She took hold of his hand. "I like you in it."

"My thoughts exactly," he whispered and went to kiss her.

Jericho cleared his throat. Remi shot him another glare and turned back to Emmanuelle. She had moved and was now waiting on the gang plank to the ship.

"Are we flying?" she asked with a wide smile.

He smiled at her. "I don't need a ship to make me fly."

She blushed at his sexual reference. He still couldn't get used to the insane energy transference that happened. It was better than any drug, but there was something that would make him happier than it ever could.

"After you." He ushered her onto the ship, impatient to get going now. "The quicker I meet your parents, the faster I can marry you."

She laughed. "Don't the sons of Lyra know how to take things slow?"

She looked over his shoulder in the direction of his brothers. He looked there too. Balt shrugged. There was a look in Acer's eyes that said slow was torture. He'd seen him around the female engineer from his ship several times now, and it was obvious to him that he liked her. Remi looked back at Emmanuelle. Perhaps speed was a must when it took so long to get the courage to act on feelings. It seemed that neither he nor Acer could move as swiftly as Balt and Sebastian.

He pushed Emmanuelle onto the ship, waved a quick farewell to his brothers and Jericho and Ambra, and then closed the door. Striding up to the deck, he focused, intent on getting out of the atmosphere and to Dazkara as soon as possible. It would take at least two days to get there and then three to get back to Lyra Prime. He could be married to Emmanuelle within a week. He smiled.

"You alright?" she said close to his elbow.

He nodded, wrapped his arm around her waist and kissed her hard, his tongue tangling with hers as their mouths fused together. When he let her go, she was panting and breathless.

Before she could say anything, he grabbed her waist and settled her down into the co-pilot's chair. He buckled her in and then hopped into his own chair. Her fingers closed over the end of the armrests when he fired the engines up and the roar shook the ship.

"I'll have you home in a heartbeat... two heartbeats." He grinned across at her.

She looked petrified.

"Take your time," she squeaked. "Honestly... I'd rather make it there and back in one piece."

"Slow?" he said and she nodded. "What was it you said about the sons of Lyra?"

Her eyes widened when he dropped the thrusters and raised the ship out of the dock at break-neck speed. He laughed.

"We don't do slow."

She squealed when he pushed forwards on the controls and they shot into the atmosphere. Before he could blink they were through it and heading out into the infinite darkness of space. He punched the coordinates in for Dazkara and then looked across at her. Her skin was as pale as her hair.

The computer announced that at their current speed the Dazkara system was a day away.

"I'll marry you before the week is out." He released the controls, letting them ease back into their auto-pilot position. "I've gone slow enough."

Emmanuelle wondered if a handful of months before getting married could be considered slow. She closed her eyes when the ship slowed, rocked and then dropped into sub-space. When she opened them again, stars were streaking past in a constant dizzying line. Perhaps this was slow for a son of Lyra. She'd made him wait and it only seemed to have increased his desire to wed her. Seeing his rush to marry her now that he could fly her to Dazkara and fulfil her stipulation was beautiful. She'd never felt so loved before.

"So what are your parents like?" He leaned back into the chair with such a cocksure air that it only made what she was about to say all the sweeter.

She turned to face him, smiled broadly and then said, "They hate Lyrans."

His face dropped.

"Seriously?" He looked hopeful. If he thought she was joking, he was in for a shock when he met her family. "So why did you join the imperial army? Don't they hold it against you?"

"They do, but I don't really care what they think."

"So why are we going to meet them?" He reached out for the controls, as though he was going to turn the ship around.

She placed her hand on his nearest one and took it away from the controls. It was his cybernetic arm. She stroked the strange rubbery skin and smiled at the way his fingers flexed, slowly closing around hers and holding her hand.

"It's tradition on Dazkara for the future groom to ask for a daughter's hand from her mother." Her eyes met his. Her smile turned mischievous. "Think of it as challenge number two... convince my mother that a Lyran is worthy of her only daughter."

"Only daughter?" His cheeks paled and his eyes widened. "This isn't going to be easy, is it?"

She shook her head. "No one says no to a son of Lyra though."

His lips curved into a wicked grin. "No one."

Unbuckling the safety harness, she looked around the bridge and then over her shoulder at the exit. A day to her home world. Remi was going to need a stern stomach to face her mother and win. If he thought battling Varkans was dangerous, he was in for a shock. Dazkaran mothers could be deadly when it came to a suitor they didn't approve of. It was cruel to take Remi there to ask for her hand, but it would prove just how much he loved her and how much he wanted to marry her. She didn't care if her mother said no. As long as Remi stood up to her, even if it was only for a few minutes, she'd marry him. She'd be a fool not to. A son of Lyra was chasing her. Remi was chasing her. It was more than she'd ever dreamed of. She'd fallen for him the moment he'd come into her office.

She stood and pulled on his hand, convincing him to follow her. His grin turned sensual when she led him towards the door. She licked her lips and smiled back at him.

"I think I need to give you a graduation present, Lieutenant Lyra IV."

He slid his arm around her waist and pulled her flush against him. His lips were dangerously close to hers, setting her twin hearts thundering with anticipation.

"Call me Remi," he whispered against her mouth and then claimed her lips, kissing her so slow that they tingled and ached for more. Her whole body followed them.

"Remi," she breathed into his mouth, her fingers twirling his dark hair around them, keeping him close. "I love you so much."

He smiled against her lips and then whispered, "I know."

She frowned and shoved him in the chest. He chuckled, his rich deep brown eyes twinkling with his smile.

"I love you too." He scooped her up into his arms and looked down at her. "I'm going to marry you."

There was such sweet determination in those words and she honestly believed that nothing would stop him from achieving his desire.

"No one, not even your mother or the entire population of Dazkara, is going to stop me. Even if it takes the whole of the Lyran Imperial Army fleet to convince them, I won't give up until you're mine."

When he said it like that, with such fire in his eyes, she couldn't wait to get to her home world and watch the calamity unfold, sure that he would be the victor.

"Remi?" she said with a sly smile.

He frowned down at her, his eyes darkening with hunger.

"Shut up and kiss me."

He flashed a grin full of white teeth at her and then dipped his head and kissed her so deep that her head spun and her hair flew up, floating and twisting in mid air.

In a week they'd be married.

She didn’t care what her parents said, just as he didn’t care what his thought.

No one was going to stop her.

No one was going to stop them.

The End

STRANDED

Captain Lyra III is known for his vicious attitude and brilliance in battle. Second youngest of the infamously passionate and handsome sons of Lyra, he's a born leader and doesn't take no for an answer. Except this time. Acer is facing a future that seems like a nightmare, a future that has shaken him and made him realise that the one thing he truly wanted in life may have just slipped through his grasp—his engineer, Stella.

Stella fell for Acer the moment she was transferred to his ship by his brother, Captain Lyra II. A year on his ship and never being noticed by him unless she's done something wrong, she's come to accept that she won't be the one to tame this prince's passionate heart, but it doesn't make her feelings disappear and doesn't stop her dreaming that she might capture him yet.

Attacked en route to Lyra Prime they find themselves stranded alone in the middle of deep space and things reach boiling point when the climate control breaks down. Trapped with only each other for company, it's not long before the truth comes out about their feelings for each other and Acer's reason for returning to Lyra Prime.

When Stella discovers Acer is duty bound to marry a woman of Lyran aristocracy, she offers him a night to remember her by, but will it be enough or will it cause them more pain than pleasure? Returning to Lyra Prime, will Stella's heart falter or will she rise to the challenge and fight for Acer? Will Acer be able to find the strength to forsake his family in the name of true love?

STRANDED

The engines droned into silence. This time, the gravity drive went with them. Stella slowly floated into mid-air in the access panel, still holding the wrench. Her knees touched the entrance of the curved tunnel, stopping her from going any higher. She wiped the sweat from her brow, desperate for a drink and some sleep, and worried that they were going to be stuck in deep space forever. It had been two days since the engines had given up, leaving them adrift in the middle of nowhere. There wasn't even a shipping lane within fifty thousand leagues of them. No one was answering the distress call.

Stella pushed off from the ceiling of the tube and drifted out into the dark, hot engine room. Turning, she waited for her feet to touch the opposite wall and then kicked forwards, propelling herself back towards the engine bay.

She pined for the stretching blue skies and Gavaelian moons of Lyra Six, the universe's foremost pleasure planet. It had been a long overdue break that she was now missing, knowing that her captain wouldn't give her the time off in lieu.

Her fingers locked around the grab bar near the Gravi-Drive. She whacked the drive with the wrench. It whined into life. Her feet slammed to the floor.

Something in the distance slammed too.

She cringed.

He had already been in a foul enough mood after they'd been attacked by the Minervan mercenary ship. It had been a miracle that they'd made it out alive with such a skeleton crew to fly the ship—only her and the captain.

Captain Lyra III.

There was no denying any part of his reputation—handsome, noble, a skilled captain, and a vicious bastard.

Not that the last part stopped every woman of mating age in the universe from trying to tame him and his passionate heart. None had been successful. Not even her.

She'd thought about it a few times when she'd first come onboard his ship. She'd even gone as far as unzipping her flight suit to expose a little cleavage now and then. After a few weeks of not being noticed in the slightest, she'd given up trying to get his attention, but she hadn't given up her feelings.

He strode into the room and her eyes were immediately on him, scanning him from the feet up as they always did. There really was no denying how handsome he was. His athletic figure was only emphasised by the tight blue and black flight suit that left nothing to the imagination. His features were noble, with bowed lips, straight nose and dark hair, but it wasn't those that had made her heart race the moment she'd met him.

It had been his stunning aquamarine eyes. They made him the picture of Lyran perfection and breeding. They made him a man any woman would want—even her. His eyes held hers. Out of the four sons of Lyra, the royal bloodline, he was the only one to have eyes like that.

He was the only one unmarried.

Anger flashed in his eyes.

Blood trickled down the bridge of his nose.

There was a cut on his forehead. He hadn't had that when she'd last seen him this morning on the bridge.

"In the name of Iskara, Engineer! How many times must I tell you to sound the warning before re-instating the Gravi-Drive?" He wiped the blood from his nose, smearing it across his forehead, and then pushed his fingers through the black tendrils of hair on top of his head to the shortness of the back.

She saluted. "Sorry, sir."

Apparently one more time. She was so used to working on ancient freighters where the gravity drive eased itself back into action much like everything else. These new Achelon Class fighters had gravity drives that snapped back on. She'd discovered that to her dismay over a year ago when she'd been drafted to the Lyran Imperial Army. Back then, Captain Lyra II had threatened to discharge her. In the end, he'd punished her more severely. She'd been reassigned to the Nephis-Lyra, his brother's, Captain Lyra III's, ship.

His eyes burned into hers.

All she'd done since arriving was piss him off. Never once had he threatened to discharge her though. He'd shouted at her plenty of times and had even personally thrown her in the brig once, but he'd never taken it any further.

What was he waiting for? Normally by now he'd be across the room and trying to make her ears bleed with the volume of his voice. He leaned against the doorway.

The gravity drive whined.

She smacked it again, frustrated. Two days and she was beginning to think she was going to spend the rest of her life stuck in space with just Captain Lyra III. She wanted to be on Lyra Six, sunning herself and relaxing. Well, she'd be on her back anyway.

"Have you tried sticking a posidriver in it?"

He held up a long cylindrical tool. A dirty interpretation of his words drifted across her mind. She swallowed. He walked across the room, steps slow and measured, moving with the sensuality of a Lyran mountain panther, and handed her the posidriver.

Her gaze fell to it and then shot back to him when he unzipped the top of his flight suit, peeling it apart and pulling it down his arms. He tied the arms around his waist. Her stomach heated through at the sight of so much bare flesh and muscle. She stared at the posidriver in her hand, wishing she was on Lyra Six right now, where men like him were waiting to do her bidding.

He crouched down in front of the boxy Gravi-Drive and the access tube for the engine. When he turned and lay on his back, his head and shoulders disappearing into the hole in the wall, she changed her mind.

Not men like him.

No men were comparable to the sons of Lyra.

She handed him all the tools he asked for, her eyes never leaving his body. They studied how his muscles shifted and tensed with each movement and the steady build of a fine sheen of sweat as he tried to fix the engine. If he was going to give her a free show like this, she wasn't going to waste it. She hoped he'd be down there a while. The sight of him like this was driving her fatigue to the back of her mind. There wasn't room in her head for it and all the wicked thoughts. She fanned herself with her hand as her temperature rose and then unzipped her tight flight suit to just below her breasts so the start of her low-cut white vest was showing. There was a frustrated growl and the sound of a fist hitting something.

"Captain?"

Acer looked at the panel above him and the flashing red warning light. He clenched his fist, causing the dark blue leather of his gloves to creak, and hit it again. The warning light went out. So did all the other lights on the panel.

"Cruskin nyaaeso!" He cursed and hit it again for good measure.

"Captain?" Her voice became more concerned.

Nothing left now but to confess. Perhaps he should've let her deal with it. He was sure she would've fixed it in the end and he'd be on his way to Lyra Prime. His family probably thought he wasn't coming. He wished he wasn't.

"I think the climate system went down."

"What?" Her voice was louder now and full of disbelief.

He looked down the length of his body to see her bent over and looking up at him. His lips parted. His breath left him in a rush. His blood boiled. He could see right down her flight suit, could see the luscious curves of her breasts. His eyes shot back to the dead panel and then slowly returned to her.

"Do you want me to come down there?"

She got down onto her knees and then all fours. She was going to crawl into the tight tunnel with him. Her breasts squashed together and her hand brushed his thigh. He swallowed at the brief contact and then shook his head. He slid out, stood and looked down at her where she knelt on the floor.

His older brother was a bastard for placing this siren under his protection. Balt had known what he'd been doing when he'd transferred her for something as petty as a gravity drive failure. Since setting eyes on her at the port of Antilles, Acer hadn't been able to get her out of his thoughts.

She stared up with him round brown eyes that gave her an innocent look and full blush lips that commanded he kiss her. Her fingers combed though her sweat-dampened long brown hair. He'd done that once. She'd been unconscious in his arms at the time. It had been barely a month ago, when they'd been attacked by the first Minervan mercenary ship. He'd received the call from home shortly after that and had selected one crew member to come with him to the Lyra system while the others had shore leave.

He'd chosen her.

It was too late though.

It was only a matter of time now before she discovered why he had to return to Lyra Prime and before he lost her forever.

"It's getting hot." She unzipped her flight suit, pushing the arms off so only a tight white vest covered her top half.

His eyes widened when she stood and started tugging the blue suit down, revealing an even tighter pair of little white shorts that hugged her hips. His temperature shot to hotter than the Lyran sun and he couldn't stop his eyes from running down the length of her long slender legs. His heart pounded.

By Iskara's wings, she was trying to kill him.

"Engineer, what do you think you are doing?"

She stepped out of her boots and then the flight suit. "I need to get this engine working and I can't do it when I'm slowly boiling to death."

He raked his gaze over her again and swallowed hard.

He had to admit, it was getting hot in the ship.

Her gaze skimmed up his legs, lingered on his bare torso, and then met his eyes.

"You should do the same. You'll boil if you don't." She gave him a small smile, one that made him believe that she wanted him in just his underwear.

It was a cruel temptation. Perhaps he should've told her why he had to return home. Maybe then she wouldn't have stripped off. If she knew it was as hopeless as he did, she wouldn't be sending out such signals.

He wasn't a prude though, and this was no time to back down from a challenge. If she was brave enough to get down to her underwear to avoid heatstroke, then so was he.

A glance at the temperature reading on the large display screens to the right of Stella revealed that it had already hit thirty degrees Celsius throughout the ship, and it was steadily climbing.

He untangled the arms of his flight suit and then unzipped the rest of it. Pushing it down his legs, he couldn't stop his gaze from straying to hers. What he wouldn't give to have had her like this a few months back when he could act on it, when he could have had those beautiful slender legs wrapped around his waist and her screaming his name.

Kicking his boots off, he peeled the suit off over his feet and then straightened. He looked at her, watching her drink her fill of his body and fighting the urges sweeping through him. Wearing nothing but his white trunks, it was no time to get those kinds of urges. She'd know the second his body began to respond and then it would be game over.

Damn his brother.

Damn himself too for not acting on his hunger and feelings for her when he'd had the chance.

He'd give anything to brush his fingers over her arms, across her stomach, and feel her silken skin. He'd give up everything if he could kiss her.

Everything.

There wasn't anything he wouldn't swap for just one moment with her.

Unable to bear torturing himself any longer with what could have been, he walked to the door.

"Continue work as long as you can," he said without looking back at her. "I need to return to the bridge."

He walked out of the door before she could respond. She wouldn't notice his change in attitude or feeling. To her, he'd appear to be the same abrupt and demanding captain he'd always been. He'd be the man in his reputation, not the one he wanted to be with her.

The corridors of the ship were quiet. He could sense the temperature had risen by another couple of degrees. The air was becoming close, stifling. It would only be another quarter of an hour before it was too hot in the engine room for Stella to work.

The doors to the bridge slid open as he approached and he walked in and down the semicircle of steps that led to the pilot and co-pilot's chairs. He looked out into the darkness pricked with distant stars. He couldn't leave it any longer.

Clenching his fists, he slumped into the pilot's chair. He shook his head when he looked down at himself. He'd never thought he'd ever be walking around his ship in only his underwear.

Sitting forwards, he looked down at the controls and then out at the darkness again. He moved his hand forwards, his finger hovering over the button. He couldn't leave it any longer. He had to send the distress call.

He'd told her when the engines had given up their fight to keep going that he'd set the emergency beacon going. He'd lied.

He'd rather be here than on Lyra Prime.

Now it was getting too hot and the situation was getting too dangerous. He couldn't risk Stella out of selfishness any longer. He had to send out the call for help and ensure she was safe, no matter what the cost was to him.

Taking one last, longing look at the freedom of deep space, he breathed a long sigh and told himself that it was only a matter of time now. This close to the Lyra system, it wouldn't be long before someone picked up the distress call and came for them.

He pressed the button and sealed his fate.

With a heavy heart, he walked back through the ship. He removed his gloves and let them drop to the floor halfway along the corridor between the bridge and the engine room. He skimmed his fingers over the dark metal walls, following the dotted line of lights that shone up from either side of the walkway. His eyes fixed on the engine room door as it came into view.

If only she knew.

She'd given him looks when she'd first come onboard, ones full of meaning and easy to interpret. She knew his reputation and she wanted to be the one to catch him, to tame him and claim his heart for her own. He wished he'd let her rather than fighting the attraction. What could have been something beautiful now brought him nothing but pain. It hurt to even think that now nothing could happen between them, no matter how badly they wanted it.

He turned down a side corridor and away from the engine room. The temperature was rising again. He wished the climate control had broken on a downswing not an upswing. He could handle the freezing cold far better than this stifling heat.

Ahead of him, the mess room doors opened to greet him. He went straight to the refrigerator units and took out two bottles of water. The cold against his skin was divine. If they had enough supplies, he'd bathe in them. Maybe once he could've convinced her to bathe with him. Not now though. He'd wrecked any chance of that.

He laughed at himself and left the mess room. A man well known for his vicious attitude and confidence had been too frightened of rejection to ask the most beautiful woman in the universe to be his. His parents would have frowned on it, his desire to marry a woman outside decent Lyran society, an engineer on his ship no less. He supposed they'd be happy now they were getting what they wanted—one of their sons married to Lyran aristocracy.

He wasn't.

The door to the engine room slid open and he stepped inside. She was on her back, her knees bent and the top half of her body hidden inside the tube. He padded quietly over to her, hoping not to disturb her so he could observe her and remember how good she looked in little clothing.

"I can't fix it!" There was a clang of metal on metal and then she slid out from the tube.

She lay on her back staring up at him.

She'd tied her dark hair back and her white top was damp with sweat around the edges. He held one of the bottles of water out to her. She got to her feet and took it from him, gulping half the contents down in one go.

"It's too hot." She wiped the sweat from her brow.

He glanced at the temperature reading. Thirty-seven degrees Celsius.

At this rate, they'd be dead before anyone found them.

He sipped his water, trying to think of a solution. There had to be a way to save Stella from this heat. Pain wracked his heart at the thought of her dying. He'd never let anything bad happen to her. Never. Nothing in this universe, not even his future wife, could stop him from protecting her or change his feelings towards her.

Stella gulped half the remains of her water, desperate for its coolness. It did nothing to lower her temperature. Seeing her captain in just his underwear wasn't helping. She swore that the second he was out of sight, her temperature had dropped by five degrees.

He was staring at her but she didn't look at him. She liked the feel of his eyes on her, trailing fire over her body and making her burn for him. If she looked at him, he was likely to look away. She hadn't realised before today, but he watched her if she didn't pay attention to him. Was he scared of looking at her when she was looking at him?

"I suggest we go to the cryo-sleep chamber. The temperature may be cooler there if we open the pods." His voice was liquid fire, seeping into her veins and stirring ideas that would only make her hotter.

She nodded and swigged her water, hoping it would cool her down.

He walked from the room and she followed him, her eyes roaming the strong muscles of his back, sculpted to perfection. His buttocks shifted as he walked and dimpled. He had a cute backside, and those legs were to die for. Long, muscled and strong, she wanted to touch every inch of them and gradually work her way up. She wished he was facing her again. There was nothing as spectacular as the sight of his torso or his body in the tiny tight trunks.

All too quickly, he came to a halt in front of the cryo-sleep chamber. The door swished open and she followed him in. It was as hot and stuffy in the room as it had been in the rest of the ship.

She stood in the middle of the room and looked around her. He went to one of the glass and white metal pods and opened it. A cool breeze touched her skin, pleasant and refreshing. She went to the pod on the opposite side of the room to the one he'd opened and pressed the button. It whooshed open. Chill air washed over her skin. It was wonderful.

She remained there, enjoying the cool air and how refreshing it was. She didn't even move when it turned colder, freezing her skin. His hand came to rest on her shoulder. She moved now, turning to look at him. There was fire in his eyes and they burned her as he looked her over. Her nipples hardened into peaks that pushed against the tight material of her white vest. She blamed the cold.

Looking into his eyes, with his hand resting on her shoulder, she felt connected to him. Her body was aflame where he was touching her, his fingers lightly grazing her skin. She couldn't believe she was standing alone with him in only her underwear. Something surfaced in his eyes that she couldn't read and his expression altered for a brief moment before returning to normal. What had he been thinking in there? Was it about her? Was it about them? She laughed internally at herself for being so ridiculous. He was miles out of her league. Her imagination was playing tricks.

His hand trailed off her, leaving her feeling bereft. Her gaze followed him as he crossed the room. It slid over his back muscles again, slowly falling to his shorts. The tight white material really left even less to the imagination than his flight suit did, if that was possible.

He turned to face her when he reached the benches near the shuttered window. His physique was stunning, better than any she'd seen in the brochures of Lyra Six or imagined in her fantasies. Her eyes delighted in following the lines of his muscles, over his smooth defined chest to his taut abdominal muscles, and then onwards to the point where they ended and the shaping around his hips led her eyes down to his shorts.

She swallowed, burning up.

"Take a seat," he said in a voice so husky it startled her out of her reverie.

She sat down on the bench opposite the one he was near. He opened the screen across the window to reveal the never-ending darkness of deep space. In the distance she could see the spiralling arms of the closest galaxy.

"It's beautiful." She stared out at the scene.

He sat on the bench and she knew his eyes were on her again.

"I never get to see it where I work," she said, feeling the need to explain.

He was looking out of the window at the galaxy when her gaze slid across to him.

He was beautiful. He was more breathtaking than that galaxy or anything she'd ever seen in her life. He made her glad she'd been drafted. The idea that she might have spent her whole life never seeing such a man, only seeing the grimy dark engine rooms of half-dead freighters and the dusty space ports of the outer colonies, made her ache and made her happy to serve her galaxy's leaders.

"It's the reason I wanted to be a captain," he said in a voice tinged with sadness.

"Your brother is a captain also." Was he so very different to his brothers?

He smiled.

"He is," he said and then whispered so quiet that she barely heard him, "he sent me you, a real star, more beau—"

She frowned, her heart in her mouth and her mind screaming out for him to finish his sentence. Had she imagined it? Had he been on the brink of saying that she was beautiful?

In the distance, the gravity drive whined.

She grabbed her bench at the same time as he grabbed his. There was a clunk, a shudder that rocked the ship, and then she was drifting off the seat, only her hands anchoring her.

She couldn't look at him so she pushed off and floated to the window. Shame filled her along with embarrassment. What kind of engineer couldn't fix an engine? Granted they were low on parts and weapons fire had damaged it, but she still should have been able to fix it.

"Are we ever going to get to Lyra Prime?" she said to the night.

"I don't mind if we don't."

She looked over her shoulder at him. He had his head hung forwards, staring at the floor. A blind person could have seen he wasn't happy. She'd thought he'd be pleased to be returning home, to see his family and the planet he'd grown up on again.

"Why?" she whispered, not confident enough to voice that question clearly.

When he looked at her, she looked back out of the window at the distant galaxy. The atmosphere in the room was oppressive as she waited for him to speak. She'd never said as much to him in her entire year of service as she had these past two days, and most of that had been today. Now she felt as though they were bordering on intimate, travelling into uncharted territory, and a part of her was frightened he'd discover her feelings and that he wouldn't return them. What if he made her leave him? Would she be happy to serve her system then?

What if he sent her back to Captain Lyra II? Seeing his brother everyday would be a constant painful reminder of him.

"What would you say to a man... about to be married?" he said with none of his usual confidence.

She didn't dare look at him as her mind raced to draw an inevitable conclusion and tears began to fill her eyes.

"Congratulations." She forced the word out through a throat tight with emotions.

Silence.

"What would you say to a man about to be married... who didn't want to be... who wanted someone else, someone of his own choosing?"

She kept her face forwards when he drifted up next to her, his hand coming to rest on the grab rail near to hers. She looked down at them, at how close they were to each other, and then up into his eyes. Their aquamarine depths were asking her that question. What would she say to him? He didn't look as though he wanted to be married. She felt nauseas. Her hand moved closer to his, their little fingers touching.

"I'd fix the ship and take him away from his future wife so he'd be happy again."

He laughed, mirthless and empty. "I wish that were possible, but I'm bound by duty... and it was my own fault for waiting too long from fear and foolish pride."

His confession floored her. If the gravity drive had been working, she would've fallen on her backside. As it was, she was shaken to the core and sent trembling. Was he saying he liked her? Her eyes searched his. There was so much fear and hope in them, so much fire and passion, and so much regret. It hit her hardest of all. He really didn't want this to happen to him. She wished there was something she could do.

"Then I'd give the man something to remember me by... so he knew that the one he'd chosen had chosen him too."

He frowned and looked pained. She raised her hand to his face and swept her fingers across his cheek, her insides quivering with nerves. His eyes met hers again.

"Captain Lyra III... if there's anything I can—"

"Call me Acer." His hand ghosted up her arm to catch her shoulder. A slight tug and she was against him, her body pressing into his. Zero gravity had its advantages.

Her hands came to rest against his chest. The feel of his warm muscles beneath her fingers sent her heart racing.

Her eyes darted between his and his mouth.

"Acer, I... every girl in the galaxy has probably said this to you... every one but me... I don't care what happens tomorrow... I just want this for tonight." She didn't know where those words had come from, but she felt incredibly powerful when his eyes narrowed on hers, filling with dark hunger, and his grip on her tightened.

He tilted his head, moving towards her. Her heart pounded, hammering against her chest as she watched his mouth getting closer. Too slow. She felt as though she was going to die before he reached her. She needed to feel his mouth on hers, his fingers pressing firmly into her sides and letting her know this was really happening.

Before she could blink, his lips were dancing against hers, sending shivers through her and making her temperature rise again. Her eyes fell shut and she surrendered to him, leaning into the kiss and wrapping her arms around his neck. Even if she could only have him for tonight, even if he was married tomorrow, she wanted this to happen. She wanted to know it was her who had tamed him and who had broken through the barriers around his heart.

His hands shifted to her sides, thumbs pressing in just above her hips. She ran hers down to his shoulder blades, pulling him closer to her and desperate to feel his body against hers. His tongue traced her lips, begging entrance that she willingly gave. Her mouth opened and her tongue met his. Electric shivers bolted through her, making every hair on her body stand on end. It was incredible.

This was what it was like to kiss a son of Lyra, to feel their strength and passion. She melted in his arms, limp and submissive. He could do what he wanted with her, just as long as he didn't stop kissing her.

He pushed harder against her and her eyes shot wide open when she began to move. She stared at the room as it slowly turned upside down and tilted her head to one side as he kissed along her jaw, devouring her and making the inferno inside her burn hotter.

Her fingernails dug into his shoulders. He lightly bit her neck and she dragged her nails across his skin, moaning out her pleasure at the floor. The blood rushed to her head. He ground his hips against hers and she rolled her eyes closed. Clearly his blood was rushing elsewhere.

She turned with him, her mouth reclaiming his, until they were floating horizontal with him beneath her. She'd never kissed anyone while weightless before. She hadn't kissed anyone in years.

Her lips grazed his before she kissed across his cheek and down his neck. He tasted salty and his heat was incredible. Even with the cool air swirling around them, he was still burning up. So was she.

He grabbed her shoulders and pushed her off him, holding her at arm's length. They drifted upwards.

She frowned and then furrowed her brows when she saw the look in his eyes. She wished he didn't look as though this was the end of the world. In all her fantasies, he'd been strong and commanding. This new side to him only made her love him even more, and was only going to make it harder to accept the fact that after tonight, she'd never feel his touch again.

She closed her eyes against the tears and kissed him again, wanting to chase away his sadness and her own. She'd promised him a night to remember her by. She didn't want him to remember her crying. She wanted this to be a happy memory, for both of them.

He turned with her again, until they were spinning towards the window. She put her hands out in front of her to stop herself from hitting it as he moved around behind her, pressing persuasive kisses along the curve her of shoulders. She stared at the distant galaxy, half aware of it but fully aware of Acer. His hands grazed her sides, pushing the white vest up until his fingers were tracing the underside of her breasts. Her eyes became hooded and her body burned, begging him to explore it and make her feel alive. She wanted him inside her, completing her and making her believe for this one night that she might be the one he loved.

His tongue traced patterns on the sensitive area at the back of her neck, sending shivers and pulses of desire through her. Her abdomen warmed and tightened, and she tensed her muscles to make the most of the divine feeling. His hands continued to push upwards, brushing her pert nipples as he removed her top. She raised her arms and he pulled her top off over them. It drifted away. Leaning backwards into him, she bent her arms over her head and ran her fingers through his hair. She wriggled as his hands skimmed down her arms and covered her breasts. He ground his pelvis against her backside and she groaned at the feel of his hard cock, imagining it inside her.

Her body hummed with pleasure when his thumbs circled her nipples and her eyes went wide when he swiftly turned her to face him. She grabbed one of the rails along the window to stop them both from floating off and bit her lip hard when his tongue swept around her nipple and he sucked it into his mouth. Arching into him, bending over backwards, she stared at the distant galaxy. One of his hands held her upper back. The other one grabbed her backside. She spread her legs and wrapped them around his waist. Her ankles pressed into his buttocks, driving his hips forwards. A satisfied moan rumbled around her throat when his hard length pressed against her wetness. She needed him inside.

His tongue tortured her nipples, stirring passion until she couldn't take any more.

Raking her nails up his strong back, she buried her fingers into his hair and held him to her breast. He suckled harder, making sparks of pleasure shoot out in all directions from her nipples and turning her abdomen hot with need.

His fingers dug into her backside and he ground against her, moaning into her breast. He ground again, rubbing the length of his hard cock against her. She bit her lip harder and screwed her eyes shut, desperate for more contact between them. He kissed downwards from her breasts, his tongue tracing the underside of it before he began to descend towards her stomach. Eyes snapping open, she stared at the galaxy again. Even if he'd kept the shutter closed, she still would've been seeing stars. His touch was like nothing she'd ever felt before. It stirred desire in her veins that threatened to overwhelm her and made her lose control until she could think of nothing but her need to feel him moving inside her, filling her up and completing her. Once she'd had him, she'd be spoiled to all and would never love another, but she didn't care. She didn't care if she never felt another's touch in all her life. She only wanted him.

Her captain.

Her Acer.

His tongue swirled around her navel and then he kissed lower, his lips dancing lightly over her skin and making her burn hotter than ever for his touch.

His fingers skimmed the waist of her tight white shorts and she sucked in her stomach when his hands met over it. He dipped his fingers inside the waist of her shorts and moved them out towards her hips. She clenched her muscles when he began to lower her shorts and her groin throbbed at the idea of him touching her there. She'd fantasised about how it would feel to have his mouth on her, his tongue tasting her flesh and her arousal. She'd dreamt of it countless times, and each time it was bliss.

He tugged her shorts off over her feet and ran his hands back up the length of her legs. When he reached her thighs, he spread them and she cried out her pleasure as his tongue darted into her slippery folds and teased her pert clitoris. It was torture. It was heaven. It was everything she'd imagined it would be and so much more.

She spread her legs further for him and he moaned. Parting her with his fingers, he licked her hard from her opening to her aroused nub. His tongue flicked it, sending fireworks shooting through her body and exploding in her mind. The desperate need to have him inside her trebled, pushing her into losing grip on the last threads of her restraint and making her mind foggy with lust.

A low groan escaped her when he traced a finger down from her nub to her opening and slowly slid it inside her. Her grip on the bar tightened as he stroked inside her, stoking the fire of her need. She clenched her muscles around his finger, loving the feeling of it inside her and imagining it was his shaft.

He suckled her clit while he pumped her with his finger, bringing her closer to heaven with each movement. She screwed her eyes shut as she neared the edge, ready to plummet into bliss, and then frowned when he pulled his finger out of her.

"Acer..." she moaned, desperate for him to finish her off.

She opened her eyes and looked at him. His eyes were blue fire, burning her with their need. She'd never had a man look at her like that before, and had never dreamed that he would be the one to do it. The blush scorched her cheeks before she could get control of herself and she cast her eyes downwards, embarrassed by how wanton she probably looked and the noises she'd been making. Her gaze slid across to his tiny white shorts and she licked her lips at the outline of his hard cock.

Letting go of the grab rail, she drifted over to him. She wanted to make him moan too, wanted him to lose control and wanted to tease him until he felt as crazed with desire as she did. Their eyes met as her fingers traced the length of his cock. His darkened and a frown married his eyebrows. His lips parted in a silent sigh. She stroked back up the length of it and then hooked her thumbs into the waist of his shorts. Within a second they were off him.

She wanted to taste him as he'd tasted her. She wanted his hard cock in her mouth, in her some way, any way. She had to feel him and know that this was really happening between them. She had to give him a night he'd never forget.

She tossed his shorts away and looked down at his cock. It jutted proudly from his body, thick and hard, nestled in dark curls. Her fingers combed through them and she looked up into his eyes. When her hand slid lower and cupped his balls, he moaned low in his throat. The fire in his eyes grew brighter. They narrowed on hers and then he tilted his head back when she lightly ran her fingers up the length of his cock. The muscles in his jaw tensed and he groaned at the ceiling.

Her fingers wrapped around his length and she gave a little tug, bringing him over to her and forcing a moan from him at the same time. Her free hand went around his back, tracing the powerful muscles there while her lips teased his flesh. She kissed across his chest, her fingers caressing the sensitive head of his cock at the same time. He groaned and lowered his head, nuzzling her cheek and kissing it. Surrendering to her desire, she let it guide her actions. She had to make the most of this moment.

Kissing lower, she moved out of reach of his mouth. She licked a trail down his abdominal muscles, delighting in how taut they were, and the way goose bumps erupted across his skin whenever she touched him. She kissed down past his navel and then looked up at him. He grabbed the bar by the window, anchoring them, and gave her a look that begged her to keep going.

Her hands cupped his backside and she looked at his hard length. She licked her lips. Her pussy throbbed. It was time she teased him as he'd teased her.

The moment her tongue made contact with the sensitive head of his cock, his hips jerked forwards.

"Stella," he moaned her name in such a hoarse voice that she was tempted to look up at him to see what he looked like.

She resisted and licked the head of his cock again, swirling her tongue around it and dipping it into the slit to taste his seed. She lapped it up and then wrapped her lips around his length and took him into her mouth. He jerked forwards again, forcing his length deeper into her mouth. She closed her eyes and sucked him, keeping her movements slow and torturous. He groaned and then growled when he tried to thrust into her mouth and she stopped him, pushing his hips backwards.

The sound of him moaning and the feel of his cock in her mouth made her slick with desire. She couldn't help imagining that it was in her, thrusting deep and slow, taking her out of her mind with pleasure.

"Cruskin nyaaaa..." he moaned.

She released him and looked up. His eyes remained screwed shut for a moment, his breathing hard and fast, and then he looked down at her. His eyes pleaded her to keep going. She smiled wickedly.

He frowned.

Before she could say anything, or move away, he'd hauled her up level with him, turned her and pinned her against the window. Her hands pressed against the window to steady herself. His front moulded against her back, the length of his hard erection against the crack of her backside. His arms wrapped around her, fingers teasing her nipples until they sparked with each flick and swirl. He kissed her neck and shoulders, sucking occasionally as he drove her out of her mind with a combination of his fingers on her breasts and his cock thrusting against her backside. She pressed backwards into him and one hand went down to her hip, holding her tight as he ground into her, groaning. Her pussy throbbed and she rubbed her backside against his hard length, loving the feel of it against her. He bit her shoulder and clamped his other hand down over her right breast. She moaned and shut her eyes when he squeezed it.

Her whole mind spiralled like the galaxy outside the window when his left hand slid over her stomach and down to her groin. Slender fingers dipped inside, the tips of two of them rubbing her pert clit and making her cry out her pleasure at the universe. He thrust against her backside, dry humping her and taking her out of her mind with need. Her whole body tightened. She was so close. She tensed against him and he dipped his fingers lower, pressing his front into her back so he could reach. She groaned at the loss of contact on her hard nub and then her eyes shot wide open when he raised her enough for his fingers to reach her slick channel. They plunged into her, thrusting in time with his cock against her backside. She screwed her eyes shut, wishing it was his cock inside her and not his fingers. She wanted to feel him filling her up and moving in her, wanted to feel connected to him in the most intimate way possible.

"Acer, please," she moaned and leaned her head back against him, drowning in his kisses and the pleasure of his touch.

Her reward was his fingers leaving her. His hands claimed her hips and pulled her towards him, lifting her slightly as he did so. She braced her hands against the window, waiting, anticipating the smooth glide of his cock into her. He didn't disappoint. He slowly eased into her, stretching her and making her sigh with contentment. His hand reclaimed her pussy and his other gripped the grab rail along the window. She grabbed it too and wriggled against him, trying to encourage him to move.

He eased out and then back in, painfully slowly. His fingers danced on her nub, circling it and flicking it alternately. Her brows furrowed and she begged him to thrust, to bury himself deep inside her and make her cum. He slowly eased into her again. It was torture. His fingers were relentless against her nub, taking her out of her mind. She tensed her muscles, clamping down on his cock and loving the feel of it inside her, even if he was refusing to move it enough to fulfil her desire for him. He wasn't going to let this be over quickly. She didn't mind. She wanted it to go on forever.

His lips played against her neck, his breath hot on her skin, fanning her face as he thrust slowly again. She could feel how tense he was. It must have been taking a lot to stop himself from taking her the way she knew he wanted to. She knew how badly he wanted it because she wanted it badly herself. It went beyond simple want. She needed it. They needed it.

He slid into her one last time, filling her completely, and his fingers swirled around her clit. A warm rush exploded through her, setting her nerves alight and making her tense her muscles around him again. He groaned hotly into her ear as her pussy trembled and convulsed around his length.

All too quickly, he had left her and she was ready with a complaint but he chased it away by turning her around and pressing her against the window. His lips claimed hers, searing her with a kiss that reignited the fire inside her.

The window was cold against her back. She didn't care. The moment he spread her legs and wrapped them around his waist, she was lost again. His eyes met hers and his cock nudged against her. She gave him a smile. It was harder to control her feelings when she could see his eyes and the emotions in them. Her smile wavered but she held it fast, trying to be brave and wanting this moment to be a happy one. Tomorrow didn't matter. All that mattered was that he was here now, and he wanted her just as she wanted him.

Closing her eyes to hide her tears, she grabbed him around the back of his head and kissed him hard, pouring out all her passion into it. She moaned into his mouth as he entered her, slow and gentle, just as restrained as he'd been last time. She kept their mouths fused together, resisting her desire to look at him in case it became too much and she ruined everything.

He had different plans. He pushed her off him, holding her close so her breasts were pressed against his chest. He looked down into her eyes, his full of so much affection that she couldn't stop the tears that filled her own. He smiled and dashed them away for her. She wrapped her arms around him, holding him and breathing a sigh when he moved deeper inside her, filling her and making her feel as though she'd never been whole until this moment.

He brushed the strands of hair from her face and then caressed her cheek.

She bit her lip when he pulled up and thrust back in. One hand went to the grab bar to steady her. She closed her eyes when he moved towards her, his cheek brushing hers, and thrust again, filling her. Emotions tightened her throat when he kissed her cheek and set a slow steady pace, moving inside her before slowly drawing out and re-entering. She'd expected it to be quick and rough this time, filled with passion and need. What he was doing was breaking her heart, making her think things she shouldn't. It felt as though he was making love to her.

"Stella..." he whispered into her ear, his breath warm against it. "Iskara no tatui sem do skiattai aishin."

Hot tears spilled onto her cheeks and she held him to her, clinging to him. She silently thanked and cursed him at the same time for saying that to her. She wished it too. She wished he could love her and be hers. If Iskara allowed it, she would be his wife and his lover until the universe ended.

His lips played gently against her throat as he eased into her, tender and slow, bringing more tears into her eyes. She held onto him, closing her eyes and burying her face into his neck, surprised at the rush of emotions that filled her. He whispered quiet words into her ear, every one of them breaking her heart and sending a warm rush through her. His body slid against hers, slowly driving her backwards towards the window until she was constantly pressed against it.

A moan escaped her when his thumb brushed over her right nipple, circling and torturing it, making her breath come faster. Her stomach tightened with need and desire, with the warmth of their love making. She kissed his shoulder and neck, unable to keep still any longer and restrain herself. He was being so open with her about his feelings. She wanted to be open too. Her mouth found his and she kissed him as slowly as he thrust into her, their lips grazing each other in a kiss so light it made her tingle. There was so much love in it, both hers and his. She savoured the feeling of him inside her, wishing he could remain there always. Another tear rolled down her cheek and he kissed it away.

"Acer," she half-whispered, half-moaned. He drew back and looked at her. Her eyes begged him to put her out of her misery, to fill her completely and sate her desire.

He thrust harder, chasing away her sadness as her desire rose to meet his. It was a divine feeling of completion, of hunger and need. He grabbed her backside and pushed her into the window, plunging faster into her, harder and deeper. She raised her legs, wanting him deeper still, needing desire to erase all her other feelings. His pelvis hit her clit with each thrust, sending tingles and shivers racing through her. She tensed her muscles, desperate to cum and to feel him cum inside her. He groaned into her throat, fingertips pressing into her backside and hurting her. The force of his thrusts increased until she was moaning with each one, clinging to the edge and ready to fall. She moved against him, thrusting back with as much force as he was showing her. He rammed deep into her, over and over until she was breathless.

She leaned back into the window and kissed him hard, her tongue tangling with his and their moans mingling as they raced towards completion. She clenched him harder, milking his cock. She wanted to feel him. She wanted to know he'd enjoyed this as much as she did. He bit her lip, kissed her hard, and stole her breath away, leaving her panting in time with him.

He groaned into her mouth and dug his fingertips into her backside as he plunged deep inside her and spilled his seed. The throbbing of his cock and his slowing movements pushed her over the edge and she moaned harshly as she came. He held her close as her body quivered around his length. She breathed hard against his chest, curling up close to him as they drifted out towards the middle of the room. She didn't want him to leave her. She wanted him to stay inside where he belonged.

His fingers brushed her cheek as he withdrew from her and she looked up at him, into his eyes. He opened his hand and cupped her cheek, his thumb caressing it softly. There was so much she wanted to say, and she knew he wanted to speak too. It seemed neither of them could find their voice now. She wished she could. She wished she could tell him all the things she needed to while she had the chance.

He opened his mouth to speak.

There was a crackling noise and then a piercing tone that made her flinch.

The communications light on the panel near the door lit up.

She looked at it and then at Acer.

"This is the Namrus-Lyra. We've picked up your distress call and we're en route."

She stared into Acer's eyes. They were full of anguish, as though they were reflecting all her feelings back at her. Her brows furrowed and she fought the tears that rose into her eyes. This was the decision she'd made. She had to live with it now. She had to be as strong as he was.

The voice came again, breaking the awkward silence.

"We'll have you back on Lyra Prime before the seventh moon has set."

Staring at his chest, her heart clenched and ached. Tears spilled onto her breasts, streaking them. She couldn't stop them now. Her dream of Acer loving her shattered.

The hot sun beat down on her. She'd forgotten just how warm the planets of the Lyra system were. Above her was a sweeping arc of purest blue. Not a cloud marred it. It gave her no peace or happiness. It only gave her pain.

Her nerve was holding, her feelings buried deep beneath the surface so the people present wouldn't see them. Acer stood before her. His entire family were behind him.

His eyes were cold as ice, his air distant. It hurt her more than anything. She could bear being parted from him if he showed her a hint, the tiniest sign that what had happened between them had truly meant something to him and that this was hurting him as much as it was her.

On the ship, he'd shown her a glimmer of his feelings. The closer they'd got to Lyra Prime, the colder he'd become, until she was left doubting his feelings and wished she was away from him. He'd barely spoken to her since their time in the cryo-sleep chamber. She hadn't been able to find her voice either. Each passing league had seen her sinking deeper into depression until she barely had the energy to raise her head. She'd spent most of the journey crying in her room. She wished she was far away and not standing here in front of him, unable to say what she wanted to and knowing that things would never be the same again.

It hurt too much to be around him now and know that he'd never be hers. She'd lied when she'd said she'd be fine with just one moment in his arms. For the rest of her life, she was going to regret him.

"Engineer Stella..." He started and his voice cracked, his eyes sparking with pain for a brief second before he cleared his throat. Was he hurting as badly as she was? The thought of that didn't lessen her own pain. She cursed him. Why couldn't he tell his parents to go to hell? Why did he have to marry another? He stepped forwards. "As soon as you fix the ship, you are to leave Lyra Prime."

She didn't want to leave. She wanted to stay right here with him, even when she knew it was pointless. In a matter of days, he would be married. His wife could even travel onboard the Nephis-Lyra with him. What would happen then? How could she bear to see Acer with his bride and know that he would never be hers?

"I'll see you soon," he said in a low voice, almost a whisper. "Enjoy your shore leave."

Tears filled her eyes and she couldn't blink them away. She didn't dare raise her hand to wipe them away. It would draw everyone's attention to them.

"Thank you, Captain."

Her hand rose in a shaky salute and she looked at him one last time, seeing the anguish in his eyes again, before turning her back. Her legs trembled as she walked to the ship, stopping at the gang plank and busying herself with the engine parts that sat in boxes on the dock. She felt sick and weak, shaking.

The scrape of boot heels on the stone floor made her turn and disappointment flooded her when she saw it was Captain Lyra II, Balt. Her gaze strayed to Acer. His other brothers were talking to him, laughing about something. Acer wasn't laughing. She'd never seen him look so solemn.

Her heart broke.

She actually felt the rip and the snap as it split in two.

Unable to look at Acer any more, she forced her eyes away. They followed Kayla as she played chase with her twin daughter and son, all laughing happily with faces full of sunshine.

"My wife plays with them too much." Balt gave a joyful sigh. She envied him and envied Kayla even more. "She spoils them."

Her chest tightened and ached again when she noticed that Acer was leaving. She watched his back, torn between turning away and running to him. She did neither. She remained rooted to the spot and forced herself to watch him go.

"All isn't lost," Balt said close to her elbow and her attention was with him. What was he talking about? She gave him a questioning look. He smiled at her. "I married a slave-girl and my parents forgave me. The moment you have children, they forget every past indiscretion."

Her heart thundered. She didn't know what to say. Was he trying to hurt her more? She was already dying inside with the thought of seeing Acer everyday while knowing he could never be hers and they could never again recapture their moment together or the love they shared. Stooping, she picked up one of the boxes and started to walk towards the ship.

Balt's hand on her arm stopped her. She looked up at him, cursing him for looking so much like Acer. Her throat went dry. She swallowed to clear it and her lower lip trembled as her emotions got the better of her. She turned away again, staring at the box. If she looked at him, she was going to cry, and crying was a pointless waste of time now. It was over.

She jerked out of Balt's grip. "There's no point."

Another few steps towards the ship and he stopped her again. She frowned at him, not caring that he was royalty or her superior. Let them throw her in prison for insubordination. She didn't care anymore.

Maybe she'd take the Nephis-Lyra and run away. She could leave it all behind her and travel into deep space, thousands of leagues from Lyra and Acer.

"Do you love Acer?"

Balt's question floored her. She stared at the ship, heart hammering and mind racing with answers. Did she tell him the truth or lie to protect herself? It seemed that Balt could see straight through her. Could he see through his brother too? He'd been watching them both closely ever since he'd rescued them.

She hesitated and then nodded. Balt smiled.

"Don't give up so easily then. Take it from a captain who's seen more battles than you've imagined. If anything is worth fighting for, it's love."

Acer stood lost in his thoughts, miles away. He didn't hear the music as it swept around him, or the excited chatter of the thousand guests gathered to watch the extravagance of a royal wedding. He didn't see the beauty of the decoration or notice that every noble and honoured family was present. He didn't feel the sun against his skin and didn't see the blue open skies above him. He was miles away in the docks where he'd left Stella to repair the ship. By now she was probably off-world and on her way to Lyra Six. Right this moment another man's hands could be pleasuring her. The thought sickened him. He closed his eyes and heaved a sigh.

He missed her.

It had been three days since their moment on the ship, and two days since he'd told her to fix the ship and get on her way to her shore leave. It had broken his heart to leave her at the docks, but he'd had to do it. He was bound by duty and there was no escaping it without sacrificing everything. He wasn't strong enough to go against his family. He was a coward.

She'd never speak to him again.

Would she even look at him?

She'd left him with more pain than pleasure. Every time he saw her he would remember how things had been and what he could have had if he'd had more courage. Every day he spent on his ship would be a day where his thoughts were always with her. He deserved to be tortured for what he'd done. It was his own fault that she wasn't his.

Now he had to pay the price.

He opened his eyes and looked at the guests. So many distinguished families had travelled across the galaxy for this event. It was all politics at play. They were only here to maintain or build good relations with his family. None of them cared about him, about the fact that he was facing a sentence worse than death as he stood waiting at the top of the aisle.

The fanfare began, signalling the arrival of his miserable future.

He looked at his family, singling out his older brother, Balt. His brother looked as disappointed as he felt. His gaze slid to his eldest brother, Sebastian. Now he knew how he'd felt all those years ago, standing here waiting to meet his future bride and not knowing who she was. Now he understood why he'd looked so pained.

His thoughts returned to Stella and he replayed the moment he'd said goodbye to her at the docks. There'd been so much he'd wanted to say to her, but he hadn't been able to with his family all there to greet him. He'd told her that he'd see her soon. He sighed again. He'd be a married man then.

His bride reached him, resplendent in sky blue and white, the traditional colours of a Lyran wedding. He looked at his future and didn't like what he saw. He longed for it to be Stella in that dress, not this trophy bride.

He held his hand out to her and turned to face the priest when she placed hers into it. He wished it were Stella's hand in his. He'd give anything to feel her touch again.

He was barely aware of the ceremony as he recited the words the priest said to him, his voice void of any emotion. A breeze stirred his jacket. He thought nothing of it. A stronger gust blew, pushing him forwards, and he frowned when there was a commotion behind him.

Turning, he dropped his bride's hand and brought his hand up to shield his eyes as wind blasted against him. The high tinny whine of forward thrusters made him instinctively brace himself. The flowers hit the floor, their vases smashing on contact with the flagstones. The guests screamed and scattered. His future wife clung to his arm and he shook her off, his eyes scouring the heavens for a sign of the ship.

His heart leapt into his mouth, hammering in his throat and making him feel sick.

The fighter descended, sending another rush of warm wind towards him and causing his bride to fall to the floor with a squeal. He didn't move to help her. He couldn't take his eyes off the ship.

The front cargo bay doors opened and the ramp descended. The ship hovered in front of him, casting a wide shadow over the shrieking guests and filling half the square.

The Nephis-Lyra.

He couldn't believe it.

Stella appeared on the ramp, her cheeks flushed and a smile shining in her eyes. There was something else there too. Fear.

"I fixed the ship," she shouted over the engines, her voice shaking enough for him to hear it. "I've come to take you away from a future you want no part of to one I hope you do."

He smiled and then ducked as the guards arrived and started firing on the ship. Stella backed into the ship for cover.

"Cease fire!" Acer shouted at the guards but they ignored him.

Anger bolted through him at Stella being fired upon as though she was the enemy. He had to protect her. He'd made a silent promise to himself that he would. He couldn't let anything happen to her. His gaze shot to his family and then to her, and then back again. He looked at Balt. His brother nodded and smiled. Had he had something to do with this? Only their parents looked angry.

By Iskara's wings, Acer wasn't going to let a second chance with her slip through his fingers. He'd said that he'd give up everything just to be with her and here she was coming to rescue him just as she'd said she would.

The guards closed in, hollering orders to each other.

He ran, leapt and grabbed Stella's hand as she reached out to him.

She hauled him up and then ran inside. The guards backed away, evidently not eager to fire on royalty. He looked down at his family and his bride.

"I'm sorry... but I've already found the only woman I want," he said to his family.

His mother stood, pushed her light brown hair from her face, struggling as the wind from the thrusters blew it around, and scowled at him. "Get back down here right now and finish this wedding!"

His father took hold of her arm, restraining her. His grey hair danced around in the wind.

"There will be a wedding within a year," his father said to his mother and then looked at him. "I guarantee it."

"But who is she? Who is her family?"

Acer turned away, not needing to hear any more. He would bring his mother a wedding within the year if his family would accept him back and accept Stella for who she was. He didn't care that she wasn't of royal blood or from a distinguished family. He loved her.

He closed the cargo doors and went up to the bridge to find her. Walking onto the bridge had never felt so exciting. He slid into the co-pilot's seat beside her and strapped himself in. She shot him a wide smile that reached her eyes, turned the ship, and blasted out of the atmosphere.

He smiled when dark deep space greeted him. He'd never felt so free.

"Where are we going?" He stared into the endless black, thinking of all the possibilities and what the future held for him now. No longer tied to a marriage he never wanted. Finally with the woman he loved. It was everything he had dreamed about.

Stella eased the ship past the defence satellites and out into open space. She leaned back into her seat and looked over at Acer. He was smiling broadly. She'd never seen him look so happy. She grinned at him, happy too.

"I still have shore leave," she said. "I was thinking we could swap my reservation on Lyra Six for Vega Three. It's a good distance away and no one will recognise us there."

She unbuckled the straps holding her into the chair.

He nodded and punched the coordinates into the ship's computer. Vega Three flashed up on the panel in front of her. There was the click of a safety belt being undone and then his hands were around her waist. He lifted her out of her chair and settled her on his lap.

"Vega Three sounds good." He brought her close to him and kissed her, his lips playing slowly against hers.

She'd missed them.

She'd missed everything about him—his eyes, his voice, his touch, the way he smelt.

Her arms went around his neck and she smiled at him when he looked at her.

"It was close. If you hadn't fixed the ship—"

She pressed her finger to his lips, silencing him.

"I work better under pressure," she said with another wide smile. She shuffled on his lap, getting more comfortable. It was a long journey to Vega Three, but she didn't want to sleep through it. She wanted to spend it getting to know him.

A smile arched his lips. "So do I. A year of you onboard my ship and finally I have you."

He dragged her back close to him, crushing her hands against his chest as he kissed her hard. She tackled his tongue with her own, loving the sensual glide of it against hers and the way it stirred fire in her veins.

She was breathing hard when he released her.

"Now I'm never going to let you go," he whispered and placed brief soft kisses to her lips.

She smiled lazily, melting in his strong arms and wondering if she was dreaming.

"Will they come after you?" She worried that they were going to be chased across the galaxy and he'd be taken from her, forced to marry his jilted bride.

He smiled and shook his head. "Balt and my father will see to it that we're left alone..."

She frowned when he looked as though he was going to say something more but didn't. There was a hesitant air about him.

"What is it?" She idly undid the buttons of his white shirt. She ran her hands inside, memorising the softness and warmth of his skin.

"My mother won't give me any longer than a year."

She frowned and pushed his black jacket off his shoulders, tugging it down his arms and removing it. He was wearing far too much clothing for her liking.

"A year for what?" she said idly, only half paying attention, and leaned towards him. She pulled his shirt open and kissed his neck, laving it with her tongue and smiling inside when he tilted his head back and to the side to give her better access. She kissed upwards and sucked his earlobe into her mouth. He moaned.

"To have a wedding."

She pushed off him, her eyes wide and her heart thundering. "A wedding?"

"You took her son away... her only unmarried son... from his wedding. She'll want a replacement one." He pulled her back to him, his lips teasing her neck and making her blood burn.

A wedding?

He wanted her to marry him.

She grinned.

"Say it again and I'll think about it." She continued to smile even when he frowned in confusion. "What you said to me before."

Realisation dawned in his eyes. He pulled her closer to him, until their mouths were almost touching. His fingers threaded into her hair.

"Iskara no tatui sem do skiattai aishin," he whispered against her lips. "I wish to be always yours and that you'd let me love you."

She kissed him softly and sighed against his mouth. "I want that too. I want to be always yours and that you'd let me love you too."

His lips claimed hers and she closed her eyes, surrendering to him completely. She knew he loved her as she loved him.

"Marry me," he whispered with urgent need, giving her the impression that it would be a lot less than a year before he wed her.

She'd be a fool not to.

Besides, now that he had her, he clearly wasn't going to let her go. His words hadn't been a question. They'd been an order, a command, a request. He was going to marry her whether she liked it or not. She smiled against his mouth.

No one said no to a son of Lyra.

He palmed her breasts and suckled her neck, alternating between kisses and playful bites. She leaned into his heated touch, melting all over again at the firmness of his grip on her and his hungry kisses.

Now she knew why people didn't say no to them.

He devoured her neck as he unzipped her flight suit.

When he was close to her, when he touched her, she only had one word in her vocabulary.

She leaned her head back and moaned at the ceiling.

"Yes."

The End

ABOUT THE AUTHOR

Felicity Heaton is a romance author writing as both Felicity Heaton and F E Heaton. She is passionate about penning paranormal tales full of vampires, witches, werewolves, angels and shape-shifters, and has been interested in all things preternatural and fantastical since she was just a child. Her other passion is science-fiction and she likes nothing more than to immerse herself in a whole new universe and the amazing species therein. She used to while away days at school and college dreaming of vampires, werewolves and witches, or being lost in space, and used to while away evenings watching movies about them or reading gothic horror stories, science-fiction and romances.

Having tried her hand at various romance genres, it was only natural for her to turn her focus back to the paranormal, fantasy and science-fiction worlds she enjoys so much. She loves to write seductive, sexy and strong vampires, werewolves, witches, angels and alien species. The worlds she often dreams up for them are vicious, dark and dangerous, reflecting aspects of the heroines and heroes, but her characters also love deeply, laugh, cry and feel every emotion as keenly as anyone does. She makes no excuses for the darkness surrounding them, especially the paranormal creatures, and says that this is their world. She's just honoured to write down their adventures.

To see her other novels, visit: http://www.felicityheaton.co.uk

If you have enjoyed this story, please take a moment to contact the author at author@felicityheaton.co.uk or to post a review of the book online

Follow the author on:
Her blog – http://www.indieparanormalromancebooks.com
Twitter – http://twitter.com/felicityheaton
Facebook – http://www.facebook.com/feheaton

18160008R00081

Printed in Poland
by Amazon Fulfillment
Poland Sp. z o.o., Wrocław